Also by C. S. Adler:

That Horse Whiskey!

"Lainey decides to show her father that she can earn money herself and that she can be as self-reliant as her older brothers. She strikes a deal with the owner of a ranch to work with a problem horse. . . . Well-developed, interesting characters; a plot whose ending is upbeat, yet not saccharine; and a convincing, appealing girl/horse relationship make this a good read for fans of the genre."

—*School Library Journal*

Courtyard Cat

"Eleven-year-old Lindsay thinks her little brother's disfiguring accident was all her fault, so she holds in her unhappiness at moving to a dingy city apartment. . . . Her gnawing guilt and anxiety provide the story with a tension that adds some prickly interest to the sweeter story of finding friends in unexpected places."

Also by C. S. Adler

Courtyard Cat
That Horse Whiskey!
Willie, the Frog Prince
Daddy's Climbing Tree
Tuna Fish Thanksgiving
Ghost Brother

What's
to be Scared of,
Suki?

by C. S. Adler

Clarion Books
New York

Clarion Books
a Houghton Mifflin Company imprint
215 Park Avenue South, New York, NY 10003
Text copyright © 1996 by Carole S. Adler

Type is 11.5/15.5-point Kuenstler

For information about this and other Houghton Mifflin
trade and reference books and multimedia products,
visit The Bookstore at Houghton Mifflin on the World Wide Web at
(http://www.hmco.com/trade/).

Printed in the USA

Library of Congress Cataloging-in-Publication Data

Adler, C. S. (Carole S.)
What's to be scared of, Suki? / by C.S. Adler.
p.   cm.
Summary: While thirteen-year-old Suki tries to conquer her fears
with the help of her friend, she meets other people who have far more
serious obstacles to overcome than she does.
ISBN 0-395-77600-7
[1. Fear—Fiction.   2. Friendship—Fiction.]   I. Title.
PZ7.A26145Wh   1996
[Fic]—dc20   95-50141
CIP
AC

BP   10   9   8   7   6   5   4   3   2   1

To my newest grandson, Thomas Martin Adler.
May the joy with which your birth has been hailed
be yours throughout your life.

Chapter 1

$\mathcal{T}$ crept downstairs and peeked around the banister so I could see along the hall to the kitchen. The room was full of bright morning light that glinted off my mother's collection of colored glass bottles and glowed greenly off the plants by the window. Dolores was the only darkness in the room. Her grim face and big body made me think of the kind of ancient idol that people sacrificed virgins and babies to. How was I supposed to eat my breakfast with her glowering at me?

My friend Allison says Dolores must be a nice person or our housekeeper, Mrs. Esposito, wouldn't have sent her over as a substitute. (Dolores is Mrs. Esposito's sister.) Allison's so logical. She can make my fears seem foolish, but she can't make them go away.

I retreated to my bedroom to call her. "Listen," I said when Allison answered. "You could have your own bed and your own bathroom if you stayed here with me while my parents are gone."

"I'd have to bring my little brother and you hate him."

"I do not." It's true Allison's two-year-old brother bites, but I don't hate him. I just don't much like him.

"Anyway, I can't talk to you now," Allison said. "I'm in the middle of painting my room."

"What kind of best friend are you?" I asked. "Don't you even care that I'm alone in this house with a woman who scares me?"

"Suki, you're thirteen years old. It's time you got over being scared of everything."

"I think it's genetic," I said. "You were born brave, just like you were born tall. And I was born a munch-kin, a scared munchkin. It's not my fault."

"I'll see you at the library at eleven, like we planned. Bye," Allison said, and she hung up on me. She often does that. She says I talk too much. On the other hand, she claims I bring excitement into her boring life. But how can her life be boring when she's the one with the four older brothers and one pain-in-the-wherever-he-attacks-you younger brother? Maybe that's genetic, too, I mean the way my life is full of drama and hers is just routines.

I was hungry, but not hungry enough to face Dolores. Dad had left for his library conference in San Diego last night. I had been in my room ever since. If I had to, I'd stay up here until he got back.

I could let Dolores think I was sick and ask her to leave trays outside my door. Except she'd probably call the doctor on me.

My best bet was to sneak out of the house and go to Allison's for breakfast. I put on pants that make me look not-so-plump and a shirt that ties at the waist and makes me look not-so-short and tiptoed back to the stairs. There at the bottom, facing me, stood Dolores.

"Oh, hi," I quavered. "Buenos dias." I'm pretty good at pretending confidence. Allison taught me that in first grade when I used to cry a lot. She said kids wouldn't be so mean to me if I pretended to be bold, and she was right.

"Your eggs that I cooked you got cold," Dolores accused me. She was holding one of my father's gourmet magazines, which surprised me bccuasc her cooking was terrible. In the day she'd been with me, she'd burned a melted cheese sandwich in the toaster oven for lunch and dried out a frozen pizza in the microwave for dinner. "Why you sleep so late?" she asked.

It was only 9:45 and it was summer vacation. "Sleeping late is what summer vacation is for," I said. Then I muttered, "I think I forgot something," and escaped back to my room.

I drifted over to my window seat and looked down into the backyard of the only house near ours. Ever since last spring, when I saw the thin spike of a man who lives alone in that house shooting at squirrels,

I've been nervous about him. I was going to report him to the police, but my mother sent my father over to talk to him instead. Dad came home and said the man had been trying to frighten the squirrels away from his bird feeder and he'd promised not to fire his gun near our house again. "Name's Auerbach. He's a computer expert type and kind of uptight," Dad had said, as if that explained the man's behavior.

"I bet he's a CIA agent," I had said, "or maybe a murderer with bodies buried in his backyard."

"Suki!" both parents scolded me at the same time. It isn't just Allison who puts down my fears.

Except for some early lettuce growing in Mr. Auerbach's vegetable patch, nothing was happening in his yard. I thought of the chocolate chip bran muffins in the freezer. Eating is such a comfort. But my hunger wasn't as bad as my fear of Dolores. How could two sisters be so different? My grandmotherly Mrs. Esposito hums Mexican love songs while she cleans and cooks. She used to cuddle me on her lap when I was little, and she's still a good hugger.

To keep my mind off my stomach until I could try sneaking out of the house again, I went to work on my current stage set. I'm practicing to be a famous stage designer. My drama teacher last year suggested I'd have a better chance at that than at acting after I kept blowing my lines. This particular stage set was a lineup of Olympic deities on a marble shelf that I got out of the downstairs bathroom when it was renovated. My deities are strictly representational. Like my model of Aphrodite, goddess of love, is a naked Barbie doll. I have her standing on a flat ocean scallop shell since Aphrodite was born rising from the sea. For Zeus and Hera, king and queen of the gods, I set out party hats with gold foil crowns. My closet's full of old stuff like that because I keep everything.

Anyway, I was kneeling on my window seat, studying my book of mythology for a clue to how to represent Apollo, handsomest of the Greek gods, when I happened to glance outside again. There in the squirrel shooter's backyard was a boy throwing a stick for a dog. The kid was in jeans, shirtless and barefoot, and the way he drew back his arm, cocked his knee, and sent that stick flying was graceful enough to take my breath away. He *was* Apollo. It was as if I'd conjured him up. Except the headband keeping his long brown hair in place was more Indian-style than Greek, and he was on the lean side for a Greek god. Whatever, the boy was real and I was struck, not by the stick, but by LOVE in neon capitals.

I dove across my bed for the phone and dragged it to the window seat, stretching the cord a little. "Allison, you'll never guess what happened," I gasped when she answered.

"What now, Suki?" Allison's voice can work like an iron pan to flatten my enthusiasms, but not this time.

"I've fallen in love," I told her.

Allison groaned. "You just got up, Suki. You can't

5

be in love already. Listen, I'm almost finished painting. Don't be late meeting me."

"Don't you even want to hear about it?"

"Not when my paint brush is drying." And she
hung up on me again. Some best friend.

I leaned on the windowsill. Now dog and boy were
playing tug-of-war with that stick. Why was that boy
in my scary neighbor's backyard? If he had moved in
and Mr. Auerbach had moved out, that would be
great, but if the kid was just visiting, I should warn
him about Mr. Auerbach. Any man who'd bang away
at defenseless, bushy-tailed creatures is dangerous.
And guns certainly are dangerous.

Well, actually the dog Apollo was playing with
probably was, too. Dogs are high on the list of things
that scare me, and it didn't help that this one was
the spitting image of a wolf. How was I going to get
past the dog to meet the boy?

I needed help, and if Allison wouldn't give me any,
who would? I eyed my shelf of old Greek gods. They
used to be pretty powerful deities, and they were dramatic, which was what everybody accused me of
being. Maybe they had sent me Apollo as a sign. I
decided to try them out.

Aphrodite was the one to ask about love. According
to my mythology book, she liked apples and pome-
granates. I could scrounge an apple from the refrigerator to offer her in exchange for introducing me to the
boy, but that meant venturing into doleful Dolores's
domain.

A glance at the clock made me decide to pay tribute to Aphrodite later and get myself to the library before Allison got mad at me for being late. First, though, I raided my closet for a plastic horse I'd gotten as a birthday present years ago. I set it next to the crowns on the marble shelf to represent Apollo. According to myth, he hauls the sun across the sky each day behind a chariot pulled by a wild, wonderful horse. That's an explanation I understand a lot better than the scientific one about the solar system with all those balls rotating on their axes.

This time I got down the stairs and out the front door before Dolores could catch me. Our dear old Dutch Colonial house is tucked away by itself in the woods on a dead-end lane off Rosendale Road. I can leave my bike propped against the mailbox post for days without worrying about anyone stealing it. But today when I stood the bike up, a dog barked. I jumped and looked over my shoulder. I couldn't see the dog because of the bushes Dad put in to shield our house from Mr. Auerbach's mangy backyard, but apparently the dog could see me. For the first time I was glad Mr. Auerbach had put up a high chain-link fence around his property.

I pedaled along Rosendale Road past the naked front windows of the squirrel shooter's dinky gray box of a house. No boy in sight. Maybe he'd gone already. Maybe I'd just imagined him. But the dog had barked. Unless that had been a different dog.

It was a good thing I hadn't given in to my mother.

She'd wanted me to go to arts day camp this summer while she was gone for a month or more in Mexico doing research for her famous author employer. Not that arts day camp is so bad, but Dad's only away for a week at the library conference, and I knew that Allison would be stuck at home. Her mother needs her to help take care of Toad, her monster little brother. I figured with Allison and me both home, we'd have more time together than we do during the school year when she's busy with after-school athletic activities like basketball and track. I don't do physical stuff. If I sign up for anything, it's dramatics or art.

I expected that Allison and I would talk a lot and bike and swim a little. I do swim some—sort of. Being "pleasingly plump" as the great-aunt I was named after would say, I'm buoyant as a seal. But now, hanging out with Allison wasn't all I had to do. There was Apollo.

I needed to plan a way to meet him. I could collapse on his doorstep and let him find me lying there in a gold-belted white tunic, which should look good with my short black curly hair. But what if he called the police? And the dog—the dog might take a bite of me before Apollo could lift me in his strong arms and carry me into his house. Yeah, that dog was a big problem.

I pumped faster, hoping Allison would know what to do.

She was waiting for me at the bike rack next to the

library, looking great in shorts and a T-shirt. That's because her legs are long and slim instead of stumpy like mine. Actually Allison's beautiful enough to look great in everything. She's five nine, with straight blonde hair and a straight nose, which she says is too long but isn't, of course.

"So who did you fall in love with?" she asked.

"Apollo," I said and described him.

She pushed open the glass door to the library, advising me kindly, "Well, before you get totally obsessed with this kid, you better find out how long he's going to be around."

My heart skipped a beat. What if he had already gone out of my life? No, that would be too cruel. "I need some excuse to meet him," I said.

"You could bake some sand tarts to welcome him to the neighborhood," Allison said.

"Allison!" I clapped my hands. "You're a genius." Baking cookies is one of my few talents.

"I hope you're not going to ruin our summer with this kid," she said.

"Me?" I flipped out my hand and laid it on one of my size B bosoms. Allison's flat-chested. She envies my bosoms, that and my being an only child with parents I can talk to who enjoy being home with me. Allison's mother's a homemaker, but she's so busy with six kids and volunteer activities that she's always on the go.

We separated in the library. I found a book of

myths I'd been hoping someone would return and immediately sat down on the floor and started reading. A few minutes later Allison was standing there holding two outsized redecorating books over my head. "Ready?" she asked me.

My room could use some doing over, too, but I sort of prefer the worn-out look.

I put one foot out of the library and stopped short. A big German shepherd was tied to the rack right next to Allison's bike. Its ears looked as tall as wigwams, and its yellow eyes dared us to approach. "Yikes," I said. "What do we do now?"

"About what?" Allison saw the dog all right, but she'd been brainwashed by old Lassie videos to think of all canines as friends.

"Allison, do you see how close your bike is to those teeth?"

"Oh, Suki, I thought you'd gotten over being scared of dogs."

"You mean because Mom made me pet that poodle? It couldn't have bitten off more than my hand. This monster could chonk my whole arm off."

"Relax," Allison said. "I'll get my bike and you wait here." She was reaching for her lock when the dog growled.

"I think he thinks you're stealing his property," I called to Allison anxiously. "Better wait until his owner comes out."

For once she didn't argue and joined me on the

steps. "That's the kind of dog Apollo was playing with," I muttered uneasily.

"Maybe it's the same one," Allison said.

"Couldn't be." I didn't want it to be. I'd *never* get near an animal that fierce. The dog I'd seen from my bedroom window had been playful—wolflike but playful as it bounced after the stick.

Allison began doing stretching exercises against the steps. She hates wasting time. She exercised while I read to her from the book of myths about how Queen Hera got revenge on her unfaithful husband Zeus by changing his various lovers into things like a spring or a tree.

"It's better than the soaps, isn't it?" I asked Allison.

"Myths are just fairy tales."

"How do you know? People used to believe in them. And all those gods and heroes were so brave." I sighed.

"Right, and you could be, too, if you didn't let your imagination run away with you, Suki."

"You always say you wish you had my imagination," I pointed out indignantly.

Allison grunted. "I never win arguing with you," she said.

"That's not true," I said. "Remember when we argued about whether you should go out with Leon or not and I said you shouldn't? You went last weekend, didn't you?"

"See, I told you, I can't win an argument with you."

11

"Well, anyway, you never did tell me how your date was."

"Nothing to tell," Allison said.

"Did he kiss you?"

"Leon? Of course not. I'd have decked him if he'd tried."

"So you're not going out with him again?" I asked.

"I don't know. I might."

Allison would never admit to liking any particular boy. She could be crazy about Leon, for all I knew. "I don't see why you never confide in me," I complained. "I tell you everything the minute it happens."

"So? You're you and I'm me. Didn't we agree we liked being different?"

"Um," I murmured. It sounded like something I might have agreed to for fear she'd get disgusted and trade me in for a jock friend like herself.

"Remember when you had a crush on the paperboy?" Allison asked.

"How could I forget?" It was last winter, and I'd awakened early every morning to dress in my jeans and romantic ruffled blouse so I could open the front door in time for the paperboy to throw our rolled-up *Gazette* at it. Once he'd whapped me in the belly hard and he hadn't even stopped to apologize.

"Then don't forget how bad you felt," Allison said. "Being in love's a pain."

Nobody had come out of the library while we were sitting on the steps except a couple of mothers with toddlers. The dog waited patiently. Allison frowned impatiently.

Suddenly I clapped my hand over my mouth to keep from yelling. It *was* the boy from Mr. Auerbach's backyard. He had come out the door with an armload of books, and the wolf dog instantly shape-shifted into a tail-wagging puppy.

"Down, Zeus," the boy said. He untied the dog's leash from the bike rack and walked off.

"Zeus," I whispered, hardly believing I'd heard right. A dog named after the king of the Greek gods owned by a boy who was the image of Apollo. The message couldn't be clearer.

"Now we can go home," Allison said. She went to get her bike.

"That was him," I choked out.

"That kid?" she said over her shoulder. "*That's* who you fell in love with from the window?"

"Isn't he beautiful?"

Allison shrugged. "If you like tall, skinny kids with narrow faces and long hair."

Good, I thought. If she doesn't like him, all the better for me. "As soon as I get home I'm going to bake some cookies," I said.

And like a Greek chorus foreshadowing doom, Allison said, "Suki, don't overdo things. Try and be cool for once."

I smiled to show I'd heard her, but that didn't mean I'd listen.

Chapter 2

$\mathcal{L}$ucky me! Dolores wasn't in our kitchen. Working at top speed, I zapped a chocolate chip bran muffin in the microwave, turned on the oven, and got out my cookie sheet. I was munching on the muffin in one hand and dredging flour from the canister with the other when Dolores materialized. She plunked herself onto a kitchen chair and asked me what I was doing.

"Baking cookies," I said, choking on a piece of muffin.

She was silent, but I could feel her eyes boring into me, and I knew she wanted me out of her territory. A voice in my head told me it was my kitchen, too, but that didn't stop the scurrying mice feet in my chest. Pretend, I told myself. Pretend. Bravely, I continued mixing the sand tarts.

Allison likes the sand tarts best of any cookie I bake, which is fine with me because they're the easiest. In an hour I had them stacked on a plate covered with plastic wrap. "Bye, Dolores," I said and scooted out of there. I had done it! I was safe and had sand tarts to present to Zeus's master. Except I had to get past Zeus to do the presenting.

What to do? I carried the cookies and an apple upstairs with me and called Allison from my bedside phone. "I need you," I said.

"Again? I'm painting my dresser now."

"You have to help with Zeus."

She sighed. "I knew this Greek god business would make you crazy."

"The dog, Allison, the dog. At the library, remember? I can't deliver cookies to that house with him there. You'll have to help me." By standing on tiptoe, I could see out my window. Zeus was lying in the yard, facing the back door of Mr. Auerbach's house with his head resting on his paws and his ears at alert. We were both waiting for the same person.

"Did you find out how long this kid'll be around?" Allison asked me.

"Long enough to read the stack of books he took out of the library." That was a guess. For all I knew he'd taken the books out for someone else, but my reasoning convinced Allison.

"Okay, okay. I'll be right over," she said, "unless Mom catches me and sends me on some errand first."

At a minimum I had a ten-minute wait. I used the

time to drape myself in a bedsheet, toga-style, with one end over my shoulder. Then I presented Aphrodite with the apple and asked for her help just in case I needed a backup to Allison. An apple didn't seem like much to offer a goddess. The ancients were always offering up animals for sacrifice. I got my old kitty-faced stuffed tiger out of the closet. I used to sleep with him until Allison shamed me out of it. Tossing beloved Tiger into Zeus's yard would really be a sacrifice. Or would Zeus prefer a bone? I could send Allison over with a bone, and while she distracted the dog with it, I could present my cookies to Apollo. Yeah, that should work.

First I needed a bone, though. My family doesn't eat meat, just chicken and fish and a lot of pasta, but maybe the butcher at the supermarket would sell me a bone. I'd talk Allison into biking a couple of miles to the market with me.

With that decided, I opened my latest library book of Greek myths. Zeus, the dog, was a lot more patient than I was. He lay motionless on his vigil while I read about Poseidon, god of the sea, and all the girls *he* seduced. Females didn't seem to come out that well in Greek myths. They kept getting carried off against their will and ending up pregnant or dead. Except for Artemis, the virgin hunter. She went around killing other people. I couldn't see myself as a hunter, though. A sea nymph would be more my style.

I was reading about how the sirens sat around on rocks luring sailors with their beauty and song, and wondering if I could make it as a siren without being beautiful, when Dolores called up the stairs that Allison had arrived. "Send her up, please," I yelled back.

"So, now what?" Allison asked, eyeing my toga. She was wearing shorts and a gray sweatshirt that had belonged to her father a hundred years ago when he'd been some kind of big-time athlete before his knees went bad.

"Do you see me as a siren, Allison?"

She frowned. "You can't sing. Sirens sing, don't they?" she said tactfully.

But I expected more than that from a friend. "Allison, could you distract that wolf dog while I give Apollo the cookies that you told me to bake for him?"

"I *thought* I smelled something good." She went straight to the cookie plate, lifted the plastic wrap, and snitched three. "How about you write the kid a note and wrap it around a rock and—" she said over a mouthful of cookie crumbs.

"Allison," I interrupted her, "when you were worried about getting on the basketball team, didn't I do my best to help you? Didn't I listen to you go on and on about it for hours? Didn't I give you sensible advice?"

"Yeah, but joining a basketball team *is* sensible.

17

Getting worked up about a boy when you're scared of his dog is crazy."

"I can't help it." I put my hand on my heart. I do that a lot. "Cupid's arrow has struck." Or was it Eros? Was Cupid Roman or Greek? I needed to look that up.

"Okay, then face the dog. You've got to do it, Suki. You can't keep avoiding things that scare you."

"Why can't I? I've gotten by for thirteen years that way. If I'm careful I could make it through my entire life avoiding scary things."

"No way," she began, but I didn't hear the rest of what she said because just then I saw Apollo. He had a book under his arm and was giving Zeus a one-armed hug while the dog's plumy tail flapped energetically.

"Look, Allison," I whispered in awe. "Isn't he adorable?"

"Yeah, I like German shepherds."

Her smirk told me she was joking. I raised my eyebrow at her and turned back to Mr. Auerbach's yard. Zeus had his front paws on his master's shoulders now and was licking his face. Uggh! Together they sat down under the scraggly tree in the middle of the yard, and the boy opened his book. Maybe he'd moved in for the whole summer. Or for good. The thought made me giddy.

"It's a great day for biking," Allison said. "We'll figure out how to get you past the dog while we ride."

That reminded me of the bone I wanted to get at the supermarket. "Right, let's go," I said to her surprise.

I whipped off the toga and changed into my jazzy neon-colored bicycle tights. How could I have been blind enough to think I looked good in something that exaggerates every curve? I covered up with a sweatshirt that went to my knees and left barely an inch of tights showing.

"Hey!" Allison said. Now she was staring out the window.

"Oh-oh," I said. The squirrel killer had come into the yard carrying a hoe and a spading fork. When he got close to the boy, Zeus stood up and his tail went down. The man halted a respectful distance from the dog and gestured with his head toward the vegetable patch below my window. Aside from the lettuce, the patch was still empty. The weather in upstate New York this past spring had been so bad we had a late growing season.

Apollo restrained his dog with one hand and accepted the gardening tools with the other, but something he said made the man's face go ropy with anger. He leaned toward the boy in a threatening way. Zeus barked, and the boy struggled to restrain him.

I pressed my fingers to my lips anxiously and didn't relax until Mr. Auerbach turned around and went back into the house.

"What was all that about?" Allison asked.

"I don't know, but Zeus doesn't like Mr. Auerbach any more than I do."

"I bet he's the kid's father or uncle or something."

"How do you figure that?" I asked.

"Well, they're both long and skinny, and that guy doesn't like the dog. He wouldn't have let the kid bring him unless he felt obliged somehow."

She was right. Maybe the boy had come to live with his father forever. Could I be so lucky?

"Come on, Suki. Let's go," Allison said. She started for the stairs.

I took one last look at Apollo, who was studying the vegetable garden uncertainly. My heart went out to him. Besides shooting squirrels, his father or uncle was so mean he kept his house lights off on Halloween so he wouldn't have to give out any candy. And considering how skinny he was, he couldn't be much of a cook. What did he do with all the vegetables he grew? He wasn't the type to give them away. Maybe he canned them, which would give Apollo something to eat at least.

We mounted our bikes at the mailbox, and I very casually asked Allison if she minded detouring to the supermarket.

"You don't want to go on the bike path?" Allison asked. She knew I hate riding on main roads. I'm not all that well balanced on a bike, so I get nervous in traffic. That's not being fearful; that's being smart. I

20

mean, I'd be stupid to do something that might get me killed.

"I need something at the supermarket," I said.

"Well, okay." Allison's agreeable where action is involved.

As we rode along River Road past the tennis courts to the rotary, I told myself that I might have to overcome a few obstacles to win the object of my heart's desire. Take Hercules; he had to muck out the Augean stable, and lots of heroes had to slay monsters. Getting past a dog shouldn't be that hard—especially if Allison did it for me.

As for the squirrel shooter, I'd be sure he had left for work before I went near Apollo.

Chapter 3

$\mathcal{J}$ stayed behind Allison as we pedaled to the supermarket on narrow roads bordered by more woods and fields than houses. After we passed Niskayuna's branch library and the town hall and entered the supermarket parking lot, I pulled alongside her and mentioned that what I needed to get was a bone. ". . . So you can distract Zeus with it while I work on Apollo."

"You're kidding," she said. "You expect me to make friends with that dog for you? You need to do that yourself, Suki."

"Me?" I did the hand-on-my-chest thing in disbelief. "Imposssssible!"

"Well, forget it, then," she said. "You don't need a bone because I'm not doing it."

"But you're my friend."

"Right, and I'm telling you—as your friend—it's time you stopped being scared of dogs."

"Allison!" I wailed in despair, but she'd pulled down the blinds.

"Well," I said in my most pitiful tone of voice, "I guess we might as well go back to the bike path then if you won't help me."

"Right," she said and promptly led off the way we'd come. The bike path was a little over a mile from my house in the opposite direction from the supermarket.

I pumped my short legs hard to keep up with her. My brain was churning even harder. By the time we turned onto the bike path, I was ready to plead my case again.

Someone behind us yelled, "On your left," and a guy on a racing bike skinned by so close that he almost unbalanced me.

"You're never going to get that kid interested in you unless you like his dog," Allison began as soon as I'd stopped wobbling and before I could start talking. "Believe me, Suki."

"What if his dog doesn't like *me*?"

"Why shouldn't it like you? Dogs aren't fussy."

"Gee, thanks for the compliment."

"Suki, don't twist things."

"Well, I can't help being short and pudgy and having hair like a poodle. I'd look like you if I could, Allison." *That* was why I'd bought those ridiculous bicycle tights, I suddenly realized. I'd been imagining I was Allison again. It was a game

23

I played, like imagining I was a movie star or a Barbie doll.

"You're too hung up on looks anyway," Allison lectured me. "Just be glad you're smart and creative."

"Yeah, thanks," I said. But what Allison doesn't understand is that looks beats smart and creative any day. People start off liking her on sight because of how she looks. Me, they don't even notice.

I don't think it's my personality, either. Sure, I get teased for talking too much and crying too easily. But I'm a really nice person. I should be accepted by everybody like Allison is, but I'm not. I don't have any friends besides her.

Allison has lots of casual friends among her teammates. They invite her to parties. If I get invited to a party, it's because Allison and I are a pair. I mean, even in first grade when I used to hand out candy in class and marking pens I stole from my father's desk drawer, kids didn't take to me. Why should they when I was the class crybaby? But I'm not anymore. What if being unpopular is something I'm stuck with for life, like being fearful?

All I knew for sure was that I needed Allison's help to win that boy.

A yappy little dog on a leash went berserk and tried to attack us as we rode past. I tensed up and hunched into my shoulders, hoping the lady at the other end of the leash wouldn't let go. I could practically feel the dog's needle teeth sinking into my tender flesh.

"You know how you always say you wish you were me, Suki?" Allison continued when I'd relaxed some. "Well, sometimes I wish I was little and cute like you. It's no fun having people expect me to act grown-up all the time because I look older than I am."

"And I don't act grown-up?"

"Well, you do, but—oh, come on, you know what I mean. I mean there's good things about you and good things about me."

I didn't care. I'd still rather be Allison than me. Like in third grade when she did the math problems so easily and got picked first for the softball team—nobody ever picked me for a team, and I needed special tutoring in math.

"Allison," I said, "it's not just how you look. You're better than me at almost everything except cookie baking."

Allison made a rude noise.

"No, really," I said. "You're so cool. The only time I ever saw you shook up was when you thought you weren't going to make the basketball team. Me, I scream under pressure and make a fool of myself in public. Remember when that student teacher I didn't even *like* left this spring and I burst into tears? I bet that's why nobody wants to be associated with me."

"Except me. . . . So do you hate me?" Allison asked.

"Hate you? How could I when you're willing to be my friend?"

"Okay," Allison said. "Good, so now listen. About this dog—I saw a TV program on taming wild animals. What you do is leave some food a few feet away from you and when the animal takes that, you put more food a little closer, and you keep it coming until you can feed the animal from your fingers."

I shuddered, imagining Zeus's great slavering jaws snapping off my fingertips. Would it be worth the sacrifice to make Apollo like me? Would he be nice to me because his dog had mutilated me? Maybe— if he had a conscience. Maybe he'd even ask me to go to a movie like lanky Leon had asked Allison. Although making the kid feel guilty was a slimy way to start a relationship, and I really did need my fingers if I was going to be a set designer.

"Your talent is in your fingers, Suki," the drama club teacher had told me when she gave my part in the play to someone else. "We'll try you out on set design." And to prove how right she'd been about me, the movie reviewer in the school paper praised the cleverness of my sets. My father had the review laminated for me.

"There has to be a better way," I said about Allison's animal taming idea.

"Not that I can think of," Allison said.

Now that we were in sight of the river, the foliage was dense and leaves shimmered like ribbons of green sequins on either side of the silvery water.

"You don't understand how scared I am of dogs,"

26

I said. "There was this terrier that bit me in the stomach when I was little."

"You've told me," Allison said. "Anyway, you know that's just an excuse. You're afraid of everything, not just dogs."

"But I can't help it. My mother says I startled easily as a baby. She says the doctor told her some babies are just more sensitive than others."

"Fine, but you're not a baby anymore," Allison said. "Remember pretend? You'd better pretend to be braver or you're never going to get near that boy."

My hands were sweating up the handlebars just from thinking about his dog. "Zeus looks like he's part wolf," I pleaded with Allison, "maybe all wolf. Okay, I should have let my parents send me to that psychologist to be desensitized." I was wailing now. "But I figured I'd get through life without close canine contact. How was I supposed to know I'd fall for a dog owner?"

Allison didn't answer me. Sometimes she'll let me go on without answering me until I run out of steam, and I don't even know if she's listening. That drives me crazy.

"Hey, Allison!" Two boys on Rollerblades came skating toward us. The one with the big grin was lanky Leon. He's an eighth-grade basketball star with an underused brain. He and his friend reversed course smartly and skated along with us for a while—well, not along with me exactly. Leon skated

27

beside Allison, and the other kids tailed him while I trailed the three of them.

"How about letting me hitch a ride?" Leon asked Allison.

"Grab hold," she told him.

Leon did, and she stood up on her pedals and pumped so fast they soared down the bike path. I hunched over my handlebars trying to keep up, but Allison and her living tail disappeared into the distance. The remaining boy glanced over his shoulder at me.

"I can't pedal that hard," I told him.

"Who wants you to?" he said rudely. And he wasn't that cute! He was as short as me and he had freckles. Even I don't have freckles.

I wobbled past him and kept going, but I'd never have caught up to Allison, except she'd stopped. She and Leon were talking to each other.

Just as I panted up alongside them, I heard Leon say to her, "So how about shooting baskets with me at the park tomorrow?"

"Maybe," she answered.

"I'll call you," he said. He grinned at her as if he'd won something and skated back toward his friend without a glance at me.

"If I'm as cute as you say, how come boys pick you and don't even know I'm alive?" I asked Allison.

"Because I'm good at sports and that's all those two care about," Allison said.

O Aphrodite, I prayed. Let there be some truth in that. Let Apollo appreciate me. Lots of boys appreciated Allison, and they weren't all sports fans. Boys had been interested in her since kindergarten, but never in me. I thought of what my father had said when I asked him if I was pretty. "Adorable, Suki. You look just like me." That hadn't been very reassuring. Dad's short and bald with a little black mustache and a paunch. Mom tells him he's cute, but she just says that because she loves him.

Off the bike path on the way home, I hugged the shoulder of Rosendale Road to let cars pass me and considered ways to attract Apollo without wooing his dog. For instance, I could get my ears pierced, wear serious makeup, and clothes that would make me *seem* tall, thin, and blonde. Or I could beg the gods to cast a spell that would make him *think* I was tall, thin, and blonde.

We had to ride past Mr. Auerbach's house again. On impulse I skidded my bike to a stop in front of it. Breathing hard, I pretended to check the front tire. I was stalling for time in case Apollo was home, in case he was looking, just in case. I had to get lucky sometime.

Ahead of me Allison turned off Rosendale Road into my lane.

Mr. Auerbach's little box of a house was covered with gray asphalt shingles, and had no flowers, no bushes, no decoration of any kind. It had squinty windows that needed something like blue shutters to dress them up. A blue door would help, too, I was thinking, just as Apollo came through the gate in the chain-link fence with Zeus on a leash.

I gulped. For a minute I'd blocked out his dog.

"Hi," the boy said to me. "Something wrong?"

I nodded, speechless for the first time in my life.

"Well, what? A flat tire?"

"I don't know."

He raised a feathered brown eyebrow above intelligent green eyes. Oh, he was handsome, with his narrow face and straight nose and lips as delicate as Allison's. "Well, so long," he said into my awestruck silence, and he started down the road.

"Wait!" Impulsively I reached my hand out to stop him. Zeus growled. I squealed in terror.

"Don't worry. He's friendly," the boy said.

I tried to smile as if I believed him. "I think I have a flat tire," I lied and took a deep breath to hide my shuddering. Zeus had fixed his yellow eyes on me, and I didn't dare take my eyes off him.

"I live in the house back there, the one behind this one," I said, and I pointed a finger without moving my hand so as not to upset the dog. The boy nodded and studied me curiously.

"I mean, we're neighbors," I said. "I saw you in the library yesterday."

Now both he and Zeus were staring at me.

"I mean," I said, "you're new in the neighborhood, aren't you?"

"Yeah. I'm visiting my father."

"Just visiting?"

"Umm-hmm," he said. "Name's Justin. Justin Auerbach. And you're?"

Zeus sat down. His teeth were still in line with my throat. I hoped Justin had a good hold on him.

"I'm Suki Price," I said. Just then Allison returned to see what had happened to me. She got off her bike and walked it toward us. "And this is my friend, Allison."

A truck rumbled by while I watched Justin appreciating her. A ton of stone dumped on my head, not from the truck, but from realizing that one look at Allison and I had lost him.

"Hi," Justin said to her softly. They smiled at each other. I'd become invisible, the way I'd been to the boys on the bike path. Starting that night I was going on a starvation diet of plain pasta. Pasta and water, period. That was going to be it for me from now on, and then I'd get myself a pair of high-heeled cowboy boots and very tight pants.

"Justin's visiting his father," I told Allison to get back in the conversation. Then I sent her a message with my eyes. I'd seen him first. I was the one who was in love with him, and he was mine. Mine, mine, mine! Even if he didn't want me.

"So where are you from?" Allison asked him.

"Colorado," Justin said.

"Colorado," I said. "Wow, that's the real West. That's mountains, isn't it? And horses?" I was wriggling my bike and myself to where I could block his view of Allison.

At that very moment a motorcycle whizzed by so close it startled me, and I jumped sideways and fell into my bike and went down onto the roadway. I remember Zeus barking. And I think I saw him leap at me, but I squeezed my eyes shut before his teeth sank into my throat.

Somebody's arms went around me. I opened my eyes hopefully, and groaned to find it was just Allison holding me. Justin was pushing my bike off the road. Then Zeus began to lick my cheek.

"Yeow!" I screamed. "Get him away from me!"

"Suki," Allison whispered. "Don't act like a jerk."

I clutched her and gasped. Justin's face registered sheer disgust as he looked back over his shoulder at me. I was ruined. Fate or the gods had done me in. Apollo would never love a girl who was scared of his dog.

Chapter 4

$\mathcal{I}$ was retreating to my room to lick my wounds in private, but Dolores loomed above me on the stairs, big as a grizzly bear with an expression about as friendly. "Where you gone so long?" she demanded.

"Just riding with Allison. Bike riding." I gave her an innocent smile, hoping to disarm her.

"You don't tell me you going."

"I'm sorry," I said. "But Dolores, don't be mad at me now. I've had an awful time."

Her eyes widened with alarm. "What happen?"

"Nothing." I had made a fool of myself in front of Justin, but Dolores wouldn't appreciate the tragedy of that. My mother could maybe, or Mrs. Esposito, who would cluck sweet nothings to console me.

"You don't go out without telling me no more." Dolores was sticking to her grievance.

"I won't. I won't," I cried and ran past her up to my bedroom, where I went straight to my window seat.

Tiger's whiskers tickled my cheek affectionately as I picked him up and held him close. My eyes fell on the plate of cookies. Justin probably wouldn't even risk tasting one now. Why did I have to be such a wimp?

I sniffled for a while over Tiger's orange and black striped head, but it didn't make me feel any better. What I needed was a project to keep me too busy to brood. I eyed my stage sets sitting on the table on the door side of the room. Some are shoe box size, like the fairy garden I'd built with thimble seats for gauze-costumed fairies made out of pipe cleaners. Some are large, like the Aladdin's cave one because I'd found a brass lamp I wanted to use that was about five inches tall and everything else had to be in proportion. The cutest stage set had a bridge made of ice cream sticks that Dad had helped me build for my troll dolls to live under.

I'd been saving paper towel rolls to make pillars for a Greek temple to go with the gods of Olympus shelf. I almost had enough to make an inner room for the Delphic oracle, where I'd use fake smoke in an incense pot Allison had given me. But I wasn't quite up to starting construction. Instead I called Allison.

The instant she recognized my voice, she said, "I'm reading Tyler to sleep, Suki. Talk to you later." Tyler is Allison's little brother's birth name. Toad suits him better.

"Just tell me," I said, "do you think Justin hates me now that he knows I'm scared of his dog?"

"How can he hate you? He doesn't even know you."

"He can hate me," I said. "He loves his dog, so it stands to reason he's got to hate me."

"You know how to fix that, don't you?" Allison asked. She's as relentless as Artemis, the hunter, or Athena, goddess of wisdom, any day.

"I'm not cuddling up to any wolves," I protested.

"Fine. Now I've got to read *The Little Engine That Could.*" And she hung up on me. What else?

If only I lived in ancient times, I could bribe a god or goddess to cast a spell on Justin to make him like me. Or suppose I could convince Justin I had the power to get him what he wanted? But what did he want? It didn't matter. I just needed to convince him I could help him get it. How, though? I had a crystal ball—well, actually it was a glass ball that I'd rescued from the garbage. It used to have a rose in it. Also, I had a crystal prism that made rainbows when the sun hit it right. What did the ancient Greeks use? Bones or something yucky like that probably.

Suddenly, through my bedroom window, I saw dark clouds roiling up for a storm. Pretty soon King Zeus began to throw his thunderbolts around. I used to hide under the covers during a storm, but I'd outgrown that fear. Now I told myself the Thunderer must be giving me a sign.

"Hail, O mighty and powerful Zeus," I intoned, "make Justin like me. You don't have to go as far as

35

love or adore, just like. And if you could keep his dog from biting me, I'd really appreciate it. Thanks."

Bang! Crash! Grrrrrowl! Some answer—loud, but did it mean yes or no? It could mean Zeus was mad at me because I was asking him for favors without offering him a sacrifice in exchange. I still had Tiger tucked under my arm. Impulsively, I kissed him between his yellow glass eyes and pitched him out the window. It gave me a pang. My father had brought Tiger back from a business trip to New York City when I'd gotten the chicken pox and couldn't go with him to see the Statue of Liberty like he'd promised me. For six years I'd cuddled with Tiger, and now he was lying on a bush getting soaked in streaming rain. King Zeus better be impressed.

Lightning flashed as I peered over the windowsill to see how Tiger was doing. I saw Justin's back door open. Zeus, the dog, came through it reluctantly, tail down. Justin's father was banishing him from the house so fast he nearly slammed the door on Zeus's tail.

Zeus turned to face the closed door and began to whine. Then he began to bark. He barked in a kind of frenzy. He sure wanted to get back in that house. Who could blame him? The sky was a furnace of churning clouds. Lightning cracked through them while trees tossed their heads about in a windy whoosh of leaves. It was as if Zeus, the god, was slashing through the darkness with laser beams. Or did Zeus know about laser beams? Anyway Zeus, the dog, kept barking.

Next thing I saw was Justin slipping out the back door. He wrapped his arms around his hysterical wolf just as the whole sky emptied onto their heads. When the rain slacked off enough so I could see again, they were huddled in a sodden lump on the back steps. I wondered why Justin's father didn't appear to make him come in out of the storm. My parents would never have left me outside like that. Unless Mr. Auerbach didn't realize where Justin was. I watched for a while, wishing I could help my hero. I could feel his misery in my own gut.

"Come eat." Dolores's voice from downstairs startled me.

I pretended not to hear. I was in no hurry to eat another frozen dinner zapped in the microwave until it was as dry as packing material. But the second time she called my name I caroled, "Coming, Dolores," and ran downstairs through the dark house. In the kitchen, Dolores had turned on every light as if she didn't particularly like thunderstorms herself.

What we used instead of conversation while we ate a packaged Mexican dinner was the radio. Dolores was listening to a talk show where people called in to reveal their personal problems to the listening public. At every awful story Dolores went, "Tsut, tsut, tsut." Her expression of sympathy for other people's trouble surprised me.

During a commercial break I dared to ask her, "Dolores, did you ever fall in love?"

"Many times."

"What?"

"I love muchos."

"Really?" If Dolores could be loved, surely I could be. "Tell me about it," I said eagerly. "I mean, about your boyfriends."

"No boyfriends."

"Lovers?"

"No. Nobody love me back." She said it calmly, as if she was resigned to her own unlovableness.

"Dolores, that's terrible!" I cried.

"Never mind." She got up to get herself some coffee. "I put the evil eye on them. Make them suffer."

"And did they?"

"Sometimes."

"Wow!" I was impressed. Dolores might be a reject like me, but she wasn't one to mess with.

I put our plates and forks in the dishwasher while she sipped her coffee and listened to a woman tell how her six stepchildren were driving her crazy. The storm had blown over. Outside the sky was purple on the horizon and glassy green above. What was Justin doing with his dog? I hoped they weren't still shivering on their back steps in the chill evening air. I could have gone outside and peered through the chain-link fence to check on them, but I didn't want Justin to think I was spying on him.

Instead I went back to my bedroom, leaving Dolores to turn to the Spanish-speaking station on the portable TV she'd brought with her to our house. I wondered if she was addicted to soap operas like I'd been until my parents got rid of our TV—not much of a sacrifice for them because they never watched it. Funny how much less scary Dolores seemed to me now that I knew her soft spot. Imagine being a grown woman and never having been loved! Now that was truly sad.

From my window I saw Justin in his backyard, crouching in front of Zeus, who was eating something. Justin's chin was resting on one knee, and his arm was wrapped around his leg. I hoped he wasn't going to return to Colorado because his father was so mean to his dog.

The back door behind him opened and light spilled into the yard. Justin's father stood there in the doorway like a large gray pencil with glasses. Zeus had stopped eating and was crouched as if he might spring at Mr. Auerbach. Justin laid his hand on the dog's head. I'll bet Zeus was growling. Allison was crazy to think I could get over being scared of dogs by practicing with that one. A cute little beagle, maybe, but not that wolf. Maybe Justin's father was afraid of Zeus, too, and that was why he didn't want him in the house.

Father and son were talking about something. Arguing? Justin stood up then, holding onto Zeus's collar. He looked as lean and tense as his father, but more graceful. I opened my window and pretended to be stargazing, but it didn't help me to hear what they were saying. Zeus strained against Justin's hold on his collar, as if he'd like to go for Mr. Auerbach's throat. One thing about a dog like that, his owner would never have to be scared of anyone jumping out at him on a deserted street. Was that why Justin had Zeus? Was Justin scared of things the way I was? Not likely. Nobody was.

I remembered how my parents had sent me to camp with Allison the summer when we were ten and I'd pretended to be sick so they'd let me come home. I just couldn't get to sleep out there in the woods in that little cabin with things rustling and shrieking outside our door. Even with Allison in the bunk below mine I couldn't sleep. Allison had said we were safer in the woods than in our own houses. But I'm not scared in my own house, just when I'm away from it. Allison, of course, isn't scared of anything.

Now Justin walked past his father to enter the house with Zeus at his heels, but his father closed the door before Zeus could get in. The dog stood with his front feet on the top step and waited. He didn't bark this time. He just waited faithfully.

***

My mother called that night, and I told her about Dolores's loves and how she put the evil eye on them.

40

"My God, Suki, did she really say that? Mrs. Esposito said her sister was reliable. I wonder if I should call and ask if there's someone else—"

If my mother had offered to do that last night I'd have urged her to go ahead, but now I said, "Mom, Dolores is okay. Just kind of gloomy and a terrible cook. But Dad'll be home in three days."

"I wish I were coming back, too. I miss you, Suki."

"Not as much as I miss you," I assured her.

"Maybe I should get in touch with Mrs. Esposito and see if I can persuade her to return sooner."

"Don't," I said. "You know how conscientious she is. As soon as her daughter's well enough to handle her own kids, Mrs. Esposito will hurry home to us."

"You're not having too bad a time of it, then?"

"Actually, Mom," I said, "I've fallen madly in love." Then I told her about Justin and his monster dog, and how I'd disgraced myself, and what Allison had said.

"Allison's right," Mom said. "You have to face down your fears."

Why did I have to be such a blabbermouth? Now I was getting instruction when what I was looking for was sympathy. "Tell me about you," I said quickly. "How's the research going?"

"Well, it would be fine if my boss could make up his mind. He keeps changing direction and discarding the material I've collected. I think he's lost confidence in himself since his last book didn't make back its advance."

"But you're not getting sick down there like you did last time?"

"No. I'm being so careful about what I eat that I'm losing weight."

"You are? I'm jealous," I said. I glanced at myself in the mirror and stuck my tongue out at the bulges. My mirror image mocked me back.

We chatted some more until Mom said, "Talk to you soon, baby. I love you."

"I love *you*, Mom." I meant it more than ever. I miss my parents when either one is gone, and to have them both gone at the same time is tough. I wondered if Justin was lonely right now for whomever he'd left behind in Colorado. I wondered if his father could possibly be as mean as he seemed. Tomorrow I'd try delivering the cookies.

Chapter 5

$\mathcal{I}$ woke up early the next morning, thinking about Justin, and went straight to my window, where I almost kneeled on the sand tarts I'd baked. Sand tarts get stale fast. They had to be delivered now or never.

There was Zeus, lifting his leg against the trunk of the scrawny apple tree. His thick, black and tan and white coat gleamed in the sunlight. Somehow I had to make friends with him if I was ever going to get near his master. I eyed my Olympus shelf. The ancient Greeks were big on courage, but whom should I apply to? Artemis, maybe, because she was a brave hunter but good with animals.

Last night I'd dreamed about a goddess who looked like Allison in a one-shouldered white robe. She'd held a spear and had a dog with her that growled at me. Probably that was Artemis. Oops, there was nothing to represent her on my shelf. I thought a minute, but the best I could come up with was a miniature metal Scottie dog, a marker from an old Monopoly set. I stood it on my shelf between Barbie and the plastic horse. "I ask you for courage, Artemis," I said. "I'm really going to need it."

It occurred to me the huntress might be insulted to be represented by a miniature when the other gods and goddesses had bigger objects, so I went through my stuffed animals and found Rudolph, the reindeer. He had a red nose, but how was Artemis to know he wasn't an ordinary deer—unless she was up on current Christmas customs. I left Rudolph on the shelf beside the Scottie to give Artemis her pick.

It was a mild summery morning, but I put on jeans and a long-sleeved shirt as armor in case Zeus attacked me.

When I went down for breakfast Dolores asked why I was dressed so warmly. "Just in case," I said. Luckily she didn't ask in case of what. I ate an English muffin while I considered whether I needed the extra protection of my down-filled winter jacket and thermal gloves. But what if Justin saw me? No, I thought. I'd better risk approaching Zeus as I was.

My resolve didn't stop my heart from thumping about like an unbalanced washing machine the minute I slipped out of the house with my plate of cookies. My brain could pretend to be brave; my body knew me better. Poor Tiger was a sodden mess in the lilac bush. I passed him guiltily and approached the chain-link fence.

"Zeus," I called, "here, Zeus."

The brute glanced at me but didn't stir. He was lying under the apple tree now, his eyes fixed patiently on Mr. Auerbach's back door. I whistled. I'm a pretty good whistler, and Zeus stood up, ears at attention. Then he slunk toward me like a wary gunman from an old cowboy movie who was expecting a shoot-out any minute. My thumping heart leaped to my throat and stuck, but I stood my ground. Artemis must be a really effective goddess. I couldn't believe myself. Well, actually I didn't have much choice but to stand there because I was too scared to move.

Zeus stopped at his side of the fence. I wished the metal was thicker. What if he was strong enough to burst through it? "Don't be silly," I told myself. "You're perfectly safe." Oh, yeah, sure. "Take a deep breath. Release it. Go." With the very tips of my fingers, I poked a cookie through a hole. It dropped on Zeus's side. He looked down his long nose at it, sniffed it, then licked it delicately with a tongue as long as a toddler's slide. His yellow eyes questioned mine. To encourage him, I said, "You're welcome." He must have taken that as a signal because the awesome jaws opened and, chomp, the cookie disappeared.

"Hey, you poisoning my dog?" Justin called in a joking way from an upstairs window at the back of the gray house.

"I baked you some cookies," I quavered. "To welcome you to the neighborhood. Do you want to come and get them? Zeus likes them."

"I'll be right there," Justin said.

"Oh, thank you, Artemis. Thank you, Aphrodite. Thank you, Zeus and Hera. Thank you all," I murmured.

Meanwhile Zeus, the dog, was wagging his tail at me, nose pressed to the fence as if he was hoping for another cookie. "Nice doggie," I said and extended one toward him. But when he thrust his black nose through a hole to reach it, I jumped back and the cookie dropped on my side of the fence.

"Now listen," I said. "Let's not rush this relationship. You back off, and I'll push a treat through to your side. Okay?" Zeus just wagged his tail harder. I moved a few feet along the fence. He moved with me on his side. Before I could figure out how to give him another cookie without getting too close, Justin showed up in a baggy T-shirt and shorts and a grin cute enough to make my blood fizz.

"So does Zeus get all the cookies or can I have one?" he asked.

"You can have them all." I held out the plate, but the fence was between us. No problem for Justin. He grabbed hold of it and climbed up and over.

"Thanks," he said, taking the plate from me.

We stood there smiling at each other. It was weird. I can talk to anyone, but all I could do was swallow and stare adoringly at Justin in imitation of his dog.

"Your girlfriend live near here?" Justin asked me.

My stomach clutched. Allison! He liked Allison. That's why he was smiling at me even though I'd been such a clown yesterday. Of course! What else did I expect? Soberly, I told him Allison lived around the bend of Rosendale Road where it got close to the bike path. "It's about a fifteen-minute walk from here," I said, wishing she lived in Alaska.

Zeus was pawing through the fence at the cookie lying on the ground. Too depressed to feel anything, even fear, I picked up the cookie and tipped it toward his teeth. He swallowed it and eyed me gratefully. I was doing better with the dog than his master.

"So what do you and Allison do for fun around here?" Justin asked.

"Allison plays a lot of sports," I said. "And we go swimming or bike riding. Mostly I like to talk and read and make things."

"Uh-huh," he said. Well, it did sound boring.

"What's Colorado like?" I asked quickly. "Is it all mountains and dude ranches like the pictures?"

"Not really," he said. "Mom used to be stationed in Pueblo, which is flat, but now she's a forest ranger up in the mountains. In the winter we're snowed in pretty much."

"How do you go to school?"

"We have a TV hookup to the school. I send my work in by computer, and the teachers mark it and send it back."

I was horrified. "But what about lunch and gym and other kids? I mean, who do you talk to?"

He laughed. "My mother mostly. Or I did until—" His smile slipped and his lips tightened.

Until what? But I could see he didn't want to talk about whatever had gone wrong between his mother and him. "Is that why you came here?" I asked. "For the social life?"

He sniffed in amusement. "More like to find out how living with my father would be."

"You mean you've never lived with him?"

"No, he moved away before I was born. My father's kind of a loner. He didn't want any kids. But I thought since I'm about grown up—" Justin shrugged. "I guess I shouldn't have brought my dog." He stooped down so I couldn't see his expression and put his fingers through the fence for Zeus to lick.

Before I could continue the conversation, Justin said, "I better get started. I'm supposed to be chopping up new ground for his vegetable garden to pay him back for Zeus's chow. Probably mine, too. My father's big on work. He designs computer software and stays up half the night doing what he can't finish at the office during the day."

"He must like his job," I said. "My parents do, too. My father's a librarian and my mother does research. But when they're home, they mostly spend time with me."

"You're lucky."

"Yes, I've got great parents—when they're around."
I took a deep breath. "So are you going back to
Colorado pretty soon?"

He chewed his lip out of shape. "I can't."

I remembered him on the steps last night, lying in
a wet heap with Zeus, as if the dog were his only
friend in the world. "Listen," I said to comfort him,
"why don't you come over and have lunch with
Allison and me after you finish with the garden?"

"Hey, thanks, I'd like that." He flashed me an
adorable smile. "And thanks for the cookies."

I scooted for the house and called Allison. "You've
got to get over here," I said.

"No way, Suki. You come here."

It turned out she was only stuck at home baby-sit-
ting Toad until eleven and could come then. I figured
three hours of digging should wear Justin out nicely
and give me time to fix him a tasty lunch. I'd bake
some more cookies, chocolate chip ones, although
Allison's not big on chocolate. But first I ran upstairs
and changed into shorts and a T-shirt. My long-
sleeved shirt had sweated through.

Don't ask me why I was going to so much trouble
to please Justin when he obviously liked tall and
blonde better than short and dark. If he only knew that
Allison thought most boys were a pain! But he didn't.

***

"Where are the sand tarts you baked for Justin? Did

you save me any?" Allison asked as soon as she walked into the kitchen. Dolores looked up from the cookbook she was studying.

"She been cooking all morning," Dolores said resentfully.

"No more sand tarts," I said to Allison. "There's chocolate chip cookies in the oven."

"Too hot to bake," Dolores complained.

"Didn't your folks get air-conditioning last year?" Allison asked me.

"Dolores doesn't like air-conditioning," I said. Allison and I both looked at Dolores, who grunted.

"We can eat lunch at the umbrella table on the patio," I suggested. "It's cooler there." I wondered if Dolores would expect to join us. "Um, Dolores, would you like some of the tuna fish salad I made? I could save you some." That was as tactfully as I could put it that her company wasn't welcome.

"I cook myself," she mumbled.

Allison helped me carry the food out to the patio. Justin was still working in the hot sun, stripped to the waist and gleaming with sweat. I was admiring his bod when I realized what he was digging. "Justin," I screeched, "those are your father's raspberry bushes."

His head jerked up. "What?"

"He just planted them last year—what you're digging up now."

"They look like weeds to me."

"Yikes," I bit my thumb in concern. His father would kill him.

Justin poked some of the brambly remains of the raspberry bushes back into the soil he'd turned over, studied the results, and shrugged. "Be right over," he said cheerfully. He wiped his forehead with his forearm and started for the house. I admired his cool and hoped he was right not to worry about his father's reaction.

"What a dummy that kid is," Allison said to me. "You sure can pick 'em, Suki."

I glared at her and said, "Raspberry bushes do look like weeds unless they have berries on them. Anyway, Justin's got real trouble. Something's wrong between him and his mother, and his father's giving him a hard time about his dog. You be nice to him."

"Sure," Allison said. "But he'd better hurry up. I'm hungry." She swiped a fingerful of tuna fish.

"Stop that, you pig." She'd messed up the wreath of parsley and chopped olives that I'd made to decorate the salad. I moved the bowl out of her reach.

"Well, if you'd cared about me at all, you'd have saved me some sand tarts. You know they're my favorite," she said.

And would you believe it? The first thing she asked Justin when he appeared on my patio, cleaned up and in shorts and a T-shirt, was, "Did you eat all the sand tarts Suki baked?"

"Every one. They were good."

51

"It's okay. I made chocolate chip cookies," I said.

"How come you didn't bring your dog?" Allison asked him crossly. She sat down on one side of the umbrella table and Justin sat on the other. He hadn't taken his eyes off her. No question he liked tall and blonde best.

"Zeus wasn't invited," Justin said. He snuck a look at me.

I gulped and said, "He can come."

Before I could even regret the invitation, Justin was climbing the fence. He returned through his front yard and up my driveway with Zeus making happy dolphin leaps beside him.

I stiffened. "Sit," Justin said and pointed to a spot three feet from the table.

Zeus sat, tongue draped casually out over his bottom teeth. Now I had a problem—how to serve my guests while keeping my eyes on the dog so I could dive under the picnic table if he sprang at me.

"Lemonade?" Allison asked. She poured some for Justin. "Suki makes the best lemonade. From scratch."

Zeus was watching his master. One ear went back. What did that mean?

"She cooks everything from scratch," Allison went on. "Cooking's one of her hobbies. The other's the theater. She makes stage sets. She wants to be a stage designer."

"Really?" Justin said. "You interested in the theater, too, Allison?"

"Me? No, if I don't make it as a pro basketball player, I'll be a gym teacher. Or an accountant like my dad," Allison said.

"You're close to your parents, too, like Suki is?" Justin asked.

"Not really. My dad's okay, but I wouldn't want to sit and talk to him all night like Suki does with her folks."

"Suki's a talker," Justin said to Allison as if I weren't there. Bitterly he added, "She could probably even get a conversation going with my father, which seems to be more than I can do."

"Do you like sports?" Allison asked him.

Zeus sidled closer to Justin and stretched out on his belly beside him. He laid his head on his paws. *Good*, I thought and hoped he'd take a nap.

Justin was saying he liked rock climbing. Allison said she'd only gone once. Suddenly the conversation got very animated as they shared climbing experiences and seemed to forget I was even there. I glared at Allison, but she didn't even notice. Why had I been stupid enough to invite her and Justin together? He'd probably have come to lunch anyway, and I might have impressed him somehow. I eyed Zeus sorrowfully. Even he wasn't sparing me a glance.

"Suki, how come you're not eating?" Allison asked.

"I'm not very hungry."

As soon as he finished his lunch Justin said, "I'd

better go dig up the right part of the yard. Thanks for the meal, Suki."

I told him he was welcome and handed him my uneaten tuna fish sandwich. "Give this to Zeus from me," I said.

"Why don't you give it to him?" Justin asked.

"Maybe later," I said.

"He'd probably eat it right now," Allison said. They both gave me knowing looks.

"He's really a great dog," Justin said. "I mean, you asked me who I talk to winters when we're snowed in. Well, the truth is I talk to Zeus a lot. You'd be surprised how he understands when I'm down or mad about something."

"It's just that he's sort of big," I muttered.

"Big and gentle," Justin said.

I didn't budge.

"Okay," Justin said. "Thanks again." And he left with the sandwich.

Allison helped me carry the lunch dishes inside. She even stacked the dirty dishes in the dishwasher while I put leftovers away.

"That didn't work out so well," I complained.

"It didn't? Why not?" Allison sounded surprised. "He's not a bad kid."

She liked him! Now look what I'd done! She liked him, and they were both physical people, and beautiful—and where did that leave me? With Zeus, of course. It would be my luck to get stuck with the dog.

Chapter 6

That evening I stood on our patio, balancing my chin on the box of dog biscuits I'd bought for Zeus while I revved myself up to offer him one through the fence. Suddenly Mr. Auerbach burst through his back door. He marched to where his raspberry bushes had been and shouted Justin's name loud as a sonic boom. Even from the patio I could see the bitter set of his mouth.

Justin's oak-colored, shoulder-length hair lifted in the breeze as he sauntered to his father's side. He didn't look scared, but I was scared for him and glad to see Zeus join him.

"I can't believe this!" Mr. Auerbach yelled. "You dug up my raspberry bushes. You're a country boy. Don't you know *anything?*"

"I live in a forest, not on a farm," Justin defended himself. "They looked like weeds to me."

"Any idiot can tell a cultivated bush from a weed."

"Then I guess I'm not an idiot."

Mr. Auerbach's head jerked at Justin's smart-mouth reply. "I'm sorry about the bushes," Justin said soberly.

"Sorry's not good enough. I'm docking you for what they cost me, which means that instead of paying you for the work you did so far, you owe me."

"You're kidding."

"Did you expect a reward for destroying my garden?"

"But I worked hard out here."

"Fine. Consider it a muscle-building exercise. Tomorrow, I'll find something else for you to do and then—"

"No way."

"What?"

"No way. I'm not working for nothing. I'll earn the money for Zeus's food from somebody else."

Mr. Auerbach clenched his fists as if he might be about to hit his son. Zeus must have thought so too because he gave a warning growl and bared his teeth. Abruptly Mr. Auerbach turned and stalked back into the house. Justin threw himself at the cyclone fence and shook it hard, but he pulled his hands away fast and began blowing on the palms. That's when he noticed me.

"Hi," I said quietly.

"You hear all that, Suki?"

"Yes. I was coming to give Zeus a dog biscuit." I held out the box in proof.

"He's such a hard-nosed—and I walked right into it when I asked if I could live with him."

"You asked him without knowing him at all?"

Justin shrugged. "He visited Mom and me on business trips a couple of times last year."

"And you liked him?"

"Sort of. He didn't say much about himself. We talked about some rock climbing he'd done, so I thought maybe we liked the same things."

"You mean, you left your mother because your father likes *rock* climbing?"

Justin snorted. "More like I got mad at my mom because I don't like this guy she's seeing. Anyway, now I really have to make some money fast."

"For dog food? I'll buy Zeus what he needs."

"No. . . . Thanks, but no. I'm not talking a few bucks." He chewed his lip. "See, last night my father made a snide remark about Mom, and I got mad and mouthed off to him. So he told me I could leave anytime, but he wasn't paying for the return ticket." Justin's smile was wry as he asked me, "Think Zeus and I can walk from New York to Colorado before snow flies?"

"Why would you have to? Won't your mother pay for the ticket?"

"Yeah, she'd scrounge up the money somehow, but I got myself into this. I'll get myself out."

"What would you do about food and shelter while you're walking?"

"I was only joking about that. The question is what can a thirteen-year-old boy do to get money around here? Other than digging." He held up badly blistered palms.

"I'll get some ointment," I offered.

"No, that's okay. He's got a medicine cabinet full of stuff. I think he's a hypochondriac."

"Well," I said. "It's summer. People need help mowing lawns and weeding. . . . Or you could baby-sit or do a paper route."

"Gerard said he made good money delivering newspapers at my age."

"Gerard? Your father?"

"Yeah. I asked him what he wanted me to call him and he said his name was Gerard, last name Auerbach same as mine. He meant it was up to me what I want to call him. It won't be 'Dad,' that's for sure."

Justin's jaw twitched. "If I'd known how he was going to talk about my mother, I'd never have come. My mom said he was a decent man, hard but decent. She never made any nasty remarks about *him*."

"What did he say about her that was so awful?" I asked.

"It's not so much what he says, as the way he blames her. Like she was the one who broke up their marriage."

"Maybe she was."

"Then she had good reason. Mom's bighearted. She gets along with everybody. He's the one who—"

Zeus nudged Justin's leg, and Justin automatically reached down to rub behind the dog's ears.

He drew a deep breath and said, "Maybe it's just as well I came. At least I see now why she let me grow up without a father."

"But she said he was decent," I pointed out. "You could just be seeing the worst side of him."

"No, Suki. He's a self-centered, quick-tempered—" Justin stopped there.

I suddenly remembered how Mr. Auerbach had yelled at me when I'd first started riding on the main road and been so scared of traffic I'd swerved onto his lawn. Then there was that shotgun and the squirrels. Justin was probably right about his father—which meant the kid needed help. "I'll ask my parents," I said. "They must have some kind of work you could do."

"Did they get home?"

"No. But I'll ask when they call me. And Dad'll be home this weekend."

"Okay. Listen, I'm taking Zeus for a walk now," Justin said. "Want to come?"

I swallowed. Did I! But would Zeus be on a leash? Justin wouldn't let him bite me, of course—unless the dog snuck in a bite behind his back. Still, to be with Justin I'd take the risk. "Sure," I said. "Meet me at our mailbox. I have to tell Dolores I'm going."

"I'll go get the leash."

My knees were kind of trembly as I walked into

my house. Besides, I had to go to the bathroom. Did Greek gods and goddesses ever have full bladders, I wondered as I relieved mine. They had sex, so probably they also urinated and defecated. Although, being immortal, maybe they could pick and choose the physical functions they wanted.

I knew they suffered from lots of ailments. Like Athena was born from Zeus's headache, or anyway, she gave him a headache when she was born. And Hephaestus, god of fire, was lame in both legs and ugly, which didn't stop the beautiful Aphrodite from marrying him. What had she seen in him anyway? Maybe he had a lovely soul. Or did souls come later?

I told Dolores I was going for a walk. She looked up from her TV program and nodded without asking me who my walking companion was. Mrs. Esposito would have asked, but Dolores probably didn't know the drill. I thought about going upstairs to put on some eye makeup and jewelry, then decided it was getting too dark for Justin to see me anyway. Besides, I didn't want to take a chance on his leaving without me.

He was hunkered down on his heels next to the mailbox when I came out. Zeus and he were leaning against one another. Like family, I thought, and wondered if I was missing something being afraid of dogs.

"I'm ready," I said.

Zeus stood up, and I took a step back.

"Want to hold the leash?" Justin asked me.

"No thanks." Zeus's eyes were amber in the dusk. He was kind of a handsome dog actually, kingly as his name. I offered him a biscuit from the box I was still clutching. He sniffed it delicately and turned away.

"He's not hungry right now," Justin said.

I was glad because then he wasn't likely to find me tasty either.

"So where are we going to walk?" I asked.

"Is there anyplace around here that isn't built up yet? Zeus likes woods and open fields best."

"Umm." I myself preferred well lit-streets where nothing could jump out at me from the shadows. But I remembered the unfinished housing development down the road a ways and led us in that direction.

The moon was out and the night was warm. The headlights of cars swished by us romantically as we walked along the shoulder of the road. Feeling blissful, I hung back behind Zeus to keep him in sight. His plumy tail waved us on our way.

We turned into the housing development and walked on the rough gravel of the newly laid out road. Only a couple of concrete block foundations were in place so far, and the skeletal framework of one house. By now it was so dark the stars were visible and that was romantic, too. What if I tripped and grabbed Justin's arm? Would he put his arm around me to steady me, and then maybe, if I leaned against him—

"So tell me about your friend, Allison," Justin said.

Pop went my beautiful balloon. It was hopeless. If I tripped, he'd help me up and go on wishing I were Allison. Aphrodite may have seen something in homely Hephaestus, but Justin only saw me as a source of information about the girl he really liked.

I swallowed and began dutifully, "Well, Allison's kind of perfect. You know—good student, good athlete, good person and everybody likes her."

"And you're her best friend?"

"Yeah. You know the way some people can't resist taking in a pathetic lost kitten or puppy? Well, that's how Allison was with me. I was a crybaby in elementary school, so kids made fun of me, and I talked too much, so teachers yelled at me a lot. Allison would give me a tissue or a candy or something and let me sit by her. She sort of adopted me."

"Sounds like it," he said. I thought he was smiling, but I couldn't be sure. "How come you were such a baby?"

"I don't know," I said. "My mother was nearly forty when she had me, and she didn't go back to work until I was in first grade. She sort of kept me close to home. I wasn't used to other kids."

"And so Allison took you under her wing because she's nice, huh?"

"And because I'm emotional and she's not," I said.

62

"That would make you interesting to her, I guess," he said.

I didn't know if that was a compliment or an insult, but suddenly I understood all those jealous gods and goddesses. If Allison had been walking behind me at that moment, I'd have dropped a banana peel under her foot. She was my best friend, but my affection for her didn't compare to the lava flow that Justin caused in me.

I was so deep in despair that when Zeus's cold, damp nose bumped my hand, I didn't bounce into a treetop. In fact, I barely noticed.

Justin did. "He might be up for a dog biscuit now," he said.

I produced one, and Zeus crunched it to bits. "You could pet him," Justin said. "He likes to be rubbed behind the ears."

So did I, but I didn't mention that. Instead, I gingerly fingered the top of Zeus's head. He was studying something in the bushes and didn't seem to mind. At least, my hand was still dangling whole at the end of my arm. I patted the hard skull lightly and withdrew.

"Relax, Suki. He likes you," Justin said. I could see his smile in the moonlight. My Apollo! But he wasn't mine. It wasn't fair, considering how hard I'd fallen for him, that he wouldn't even totter slightly for me.

"I'm scared of dogs," I said softly.

"No kidding!" Justin's lips twitched with amusement.

O Aphrodite, O Artemis, O Athena, why make me find him so adorable when I couldn't have him?

Half an hour later I dragged into the house, exhausted from my stormy feelings. Dolores was still in the kitchen, sitting in the same chair in front of her TV, watching a sitcom.

"Dolores," I said, "how do you stand it?"

"What?"

"Life."

"It's hard," she said.

"You can say that again."

"I got to go back and take care of my old father. Run, run, run. He don't give me no rest. I like to stay here and let my sister do it."

I shuddered. Oh no! Dolores wanted to switch jobs with Mrs. Esposito, my lovable Mrs. Esposito. To be stuck with Dolores forever would be a terrible fate. Not only was she the worst cook I'd ever met, but she wasn't doing any of the housework that Mrs. Esposito did so efficiently.

". . . 'You take care of him,' my mother said to me before she died," Dolores was saying. "Because my sister, she got married, and my brothers they married and moved away, and my father he had a job then, and I was the youngest. So now I feed him and bathe him. And he is heavy and he soils himself. I never get done."

She shook her head. Her dark eyes hung themselves on mine. "My sister called. She comes back Monday. She wanted to speak to you, but I told her you were walking with a boy. She said it is too late. I said you don't get in any trouble."

I wondered how Dolores had known it was a boy I had gone off with, but I didn't ask. Maybe she spied out of windows like I did. "You don't have to worry," I said. "He's interested in my friend, Allison, not me."

"Tsut, tsut, tsut," Dolores said as if I were one of her talk show unfortunates.

We exchanged glances of understanding. For a moment Dolores was me and I was Dolores. Not really, though. I had wonderful, live, healthy parents. I wasn't beautiful, but there was a chance I might improve when I grew up. Dolores, on the other hand, was stuck with what she was.

"Don't worry about breakfast tomorrow morning, Dolores," I said. "You can sleep in and I'll get my own."

Dolores nodded and smiled for the first time ever. At least she had beautiful teeth.

Chapter 7

*J*t was raining hard the next morning, so I lay in bed daydreaming until ten. I had just gotten dressed when the doorbell rang. While Dolores opened the front door, I ran a brush through my curls in case it was Justin. But when I looked down the stairs at our entry hall, there in the doorway talking to Dolores was not Justin or Allison but Mr. Auerbach. I nearly fainted from shock.

"Is something wrong?" I called down. Because why should Justin's father be there unless something had happened to Justin?

Dolores turned to look up at me. "He wants to know where his son is."

"I don't know," I said.

Mr. Auerbach was bareheaded. Rain dripped off the end of his nose, and the shoulders of his suit jacket were soaked. "Justin didn't come here?" he asked me.

"Not as far as I know. I just got up."

"He doesn't know anybody else." The man's lean jaw worked tensely. "If he's not here, I don't know where to look for him."

"You think Justin ran away?" I asked.

Mr. Auerbach's eyes squinted at me painfully. "His room's empty. His things are gone."

"Maybe he's just out walking Zeus."

"The dog's still in the yard." Mr. Auerbach rubbed his forehead with trembling fingers. I couldn't believe this was the same man I'd feared. He didn't look capable of shooting a squirrel now.

Dolores must have been noticing how pitiful he was, too, because she suddenly said, "I make you a cup of coffee," and stepped aside to let him into our house.

"No. No, thank you. But if you see him, would you tell him—" His eyes met mine, and he pressed his lips together as if he couldn't say the words, or maybe didn't have any. "Tell him I'm—I'm looking for him."

"Sure, I'll tell him," I said.

Mr. Auerbach thanked me with automatic politeness and abruptly turned and walked back out into the rain. I hoped he didn't go to work in that wet suit jacket.

"Where his son go?" Dolores asked me.

"Beats me," I said. Unless he had gone to Allison's. Except he didn't know where she lived. Or did he?

"He wouldn't leave his dog behind," Dolores said.

"No," I said, "that's for sure. But his father seemed really worried about him. Do you think—" I was beginning to wonder if their not getting along *had* been all Mr. Auerbach's fault. "He didn't seem so mean, did he?"

Dolores rolled her lower lip out. "He don't look like an easy man to live with," she said.

∗∗∗

Allison and I play board games on rainy days. It's something I love and she tolerates. After breakfast, I donned my red plastic raincoat and set off for her house. I got as far as my bike, which was leaning on the lamppost as usual, when Justin appeared at the end of my lane. "Where were you?" I asked. "Your father came looking for you."

"He did? I thought he'd be glad to find me gone. I just went down the road to ask those people moving in if they wanted to hire me for anything. And then I checked out a guy I saw building a patio yesterday."

"Any luck?"

"No. . . . I better call my father. This wouldn't be a great day to move into the woods, and that's what I was planning."

"It's a great day to be indoors. Do you want to come to Allison's with me?" I asked impulsively.

"Sure," he said. "Mind if I call my father from your house first?"

I didn't mind. I followed him to the kitchen, surprised to find it strangely empty, without Dolores's somber presence. Justin picked up the phone and I waited, annoyed with myself for not thinking fast enough to make a change in plans and invite him to play chess with me at my house. True, I'm a terrible chess player. Well, then Scrabble, or even dominoes. Allison wouldn't have cared if I'd told her I wasn't coming. And then I'd have had Justin to myself. This way I'd just given him another chance to be wowed by Allison.

There was an unfamiliar duffle bag on our covered patio. I guessed it was Justin's and was glad his father hadn't seen it.

". . . Yeah, I'm going," I heard him say into the receiver. "But it's not a good day for traveling. . . . Okay, sure. Yeah, that'd be good." He hung up and shook his head. "I can't figure him. He says it's supposed to clear up later and he's bringing home a steak to grill outside. After the things we said to each other—I don't know, but it sounds like he wants to try again."

"So?"

"So, I'm willing," Justin said. "By the way, I stowed my belongings on your patio for safekeeping this morning. If I can leave them there, I'll get Zeus and we'll go to Allison's."

"Ah," I said and swallowed. My quivery nerve endings mustn't have gotten the message about not being afraid of Zeus anymore. "Do you think we should take the dog? I mean, Allison's little brother—"

"Zeus is good with little kids."

"This one screams and pinches."

"Don't worry. Zeus will do fine."

I didn't admit that it wasn't really Toad I was worried about. But the second time I switched sides to avoid being on the same one as Zeus, Justin said, "You still don't trust him, do you, Suki?"

"Sure, I do," I said, trying to block out my memory of Zeus baring his teeth at Mr. Auerbach.

Biking to Allison's takes me about five minutes, but Justin had been using his father's bike and it was locked in a toolshed. So we walked the couple of miles along Rosendale Road, past the bend where it runs parallel to the river. Along there it's mostly just maple, oak, and birch woods with a few old houses set on acres of land.

There was only a sifting of rain left by the time we got to the bridge over the brook. We stopped to admire the rush of swollen water over the rocky streambed beneath us, and I unbuttoned my Little Red Riding Hood raincoat, glad that I'd put on a skirt that morning. Skirts are slimming.

"It's pretty around here," Justin said.

"You think so? But not compared to where you live in Colorado, right?"

"I don't know about that. After the snow melts in June, everything's mud, and the summers are short.

It's a lot better than where we were stationed in Wyoming, though. *Nothing* grew there. Too much wind."

"You really have lived in interesting places."

He laughed. "I'd say this place is interesting. I like being able to bike to the library. It'd be fun going to school here."

"Oh, it is," I agreed eagerly and told him that when my father called last night, I'd asked about work for Justin. "Unfortunately, Dad likes our gardening service," I said, and then I had an inspiration. "But you might be able to help him clean out our garage."

"Sure, I'd be glad to."

I hoped Dad would go for the idea, too. He's been talking about cleaning out the garage forever. Maybe if I offered to do it for him with Justin's help, he'd agree.

Justin was wet through, but the air was warm and he didn't seem to mind. We stopped to let Zeus relieve himself. This time of day the traffic was only about a car a minute.

I could have kept hiking with Justin forever, but all too soon I spotted the high pitched roof of Allison's two-hundred-year-old farmhouse with its four chimneys. It was time to prepare Justin for Toad.

"See, Allison's parents were pretty old when they had him," I explained, "and they don't have the energy to deal with him. I mean, you'd need a whip and a chair to handle that kid."

"I'm here, you guys," Allison called to us from her

front porch, not the least bit fazed by my bringing Justin with me. "Tell me what you want to play and I'll bring it to the patio in back." Allison had every board game ever made, mostly inherited from her two grown-up brothers, who'd married and moved away. Her sixteen-year-old twin brothers never played with anything that wasn't electronic.

We circled from the driveway around the old cellar entrance to the back of the house, where there was a covered patio with a redwood picnic table and chairs. In the summertime that was where Allison and I always played. She hates being indoors.

The sun broke through the clouds for a moment, and the moist air was so sweet we seemed to be breathing nectar. Allison looked gorgeous as usual in a wrinkled man's shirt with the sleeves rolled up. I took off my raincoat. Justin didn't even look at my red and white striped skirt; he was too busy grinning at Allison and drying himself with the beach towel she had handed him. I didn't like the way their hands touched when he handed the towel back to her. Meanwhile, Zeus was spraying me with water as he shook himself dry.

I backed away from the dog, my eyes on Allison and Justin, and bumped into Toad. He had come around the house and was pedaling his tricyle in circles on the patio. Toad promptly turned and tried to ram Zeus, who knocked over a geranium getting out of the away. The pot broke.

"Oh, boy, I'm sorry," Justin said.

"No problem," Allison said. "I'll repot it later."

Toad took another pass at Zeus, who backed out into the rain. It had started up again.

"Hey you, kid. Come here," Justin ordered. He was squatting on his heels and he locked eyes with Toad, who turned to pedal off. Before Toad could escape, Justin stood up and grabbed him. He hoisted Toad up by his elbows so that they were eye to eye.

"You know you almost hurt my dog? I think you should apologize," Justin said.

"Let go." Toad kicked Justin. Fortunately he was bare-toed in sandals.

"I'll let you go when you tell me how sorry you are," Justin said. Toad hung limply, with an expression as ugly as his nickname. Next Justin tied him into a complicated knot that captured both his arms and legs. The only thing Toad could move was his head.

"Watch out," Allison yelled as Toad's teeth descended.

Before the teeth reached Justin's arm, Zeus growled menacingly and Justin hung Toad upside down. Again Justin asked, "Can you say, 'I'm sorry, Justin'?"

"No."

"Oh? You like being upside down?"

"Want soda or juice?" Allison asked me calmly. Subduing her little brother could be depended on to take a while.

"Cranberry soda if you have it," I said.

"Sounds good," Justin told her.

She left, and I sat down at the redwood picnic table. Toad was getting very red in the face. "I'm waiting, kid," Justin said patiently.

"Sorry," Toad squeaked.

Immediately Justin turned him right side up and said, "That's a nice trike you've got there. Can I ride it?"

"No!" Toad reseated himself and rode off into the rain as far as he could get on the mowed part of the yard.

Zeus had been sitting on his haunches watching the action. "It's okay now, Zeus," Justin told him. As if he understood, Zeus lay down with his head on his paws.

"You westerners sure know how to deal with desperadoes," I said.

Justin grinned. "My mom says I was a stubborn little kid myself."

I didn't believe it. My Apollo could never have been like Toad.

"Here's Stratego, Risk, and Life," Allison said. "I didn't bring out any word games because Suki'll just beat us at those."

"I'm pretty good at word games myself," Justin said.

Allison groaned and went back for Boggle, which is the only word game she wins occasionally. Toad reentered the patio and let Justin, not me, dry him off. When he leaned against Justin's knee and reached out to pet Zeus, I yelped, fearful he might lose his grubby little fingers.

"Suki!" Justin reproved me.

"Sorry," I said. Meanwhile Toad was pulling Zeus's ear and getting his cheek licked in return.

"Nice doggie," Toad said. He and Zeus retired to the sandbox side of the patio, which was full of construction toys.

While Zeus baby-sat for us, we three played Boggle. Justin and I divided the wins between us until Allison said, "I'm sick of this game. I hate losing."

"You don't look like a girl who loses at much," Justin said. The admiration in his eyes sliced my heart in two.

We stopped playing and just talked for a while. It turned out Justin and his mother played Boggle on long winter evenings when they got tired of Scrabble.

"I guess being an only child has some advantages," I said, mostly to point out that Justin and I had that in common.

"Do you get everything you want like Suki does?" Allison asked him.

I could have killed her. "I don't get everything I want," I protested.

"Sure you do," Allison said. "Just because you don't want much doesn't make me less jealous."

"I guess I don't want much either," Justin said. "Except right now the money for a plane ticket home."

"You don't think you're going to make peace with your father over the grill tonight?" I asked.

He smiled. "I don't know, Suki. But just in case, can someone tell me where I could camp out around here?"

"There's a great spot on the back of our property you could use," Allison said. Her family owned the woods all the way back to the bike path, which was built where the railroad tracks used to run along the riverbank. Allison's family doesn't do anything with those acres. In fact, they've let the trees grow so tall their view of the river is blocked.

"Maybe we could do a camp-out together, the three of us," Allison said.

She looked right at me then, the traitor.

"Hey, that'd be fun," Justin said immediately.

"Fun," I repeated, shuddering. Out there in the woods, with only a sleeping bag between me and the elements, awful things could happen. A bear might step on me, or I could be attacked by a crazy person, or hit by sudden lightning, or eaten alive by mosquitoes.

"How about it, Suki? Would you do it?" Allison was challenging me, and right in front of Justin. How could she? She knew I'd been scared of the woods at night ever since our camping experience when we were ten. I'd gotten so hysterical then that I'd made my parents come and get me. Allison's been trying to make me sleep out under the stars

76

ever since. I've gone on sunset walks with her on the bikepath, but as soon as it begins to get dark, I race home. Not that I'm so scared of the dark itself; it's that things can hide in it.

I was pawing about for an excuse when I happened to see an exchange of looks between Allison and Justin. O Aphrodite help me. O Artemis, O anybody. Please help me wipe that smirk off their faces. "Sure," I said breathlessly, "Sure, I'll do it."

"Hurray!" Allison said, and she clapped for me.

While I was glaring at her, Justin gestured at the grass in the backyard, which was overdue for a haircut. "Do your folks need someone to mow the lawn, Allison?"

"That's my brother Eric's job," Allison said, "but he's busy organizing a band. I offered to mow myself—Mom pays well—but my father doesn't trust me with machinery. He wouldn't let me use his power saw when I wanted to make a bookcase for my room, either."

"I need to earn some money really bad," Justin said. He was apparently not expecting much from the father-son barbecue night.

"Well, I'll ask Eric if he wants to hire someone to do the job for him," Allison said.

Toad came and leaned on her knee. "Go potty."

"Okay. Let's go," Allison said, and she led Toad off into the house.

Justin was telling me about how much his mother

liked camping when Allison came tearing back out. "Can you believe that brother of mine?"

"Toad?" I asked.

"Eric. He called to leave a message that he's going somewhere with his girlfriend, and I asked him about the lawn and he said, sure. He'd pay eight dollars and to show him how the machine works."

"Great!" Justin stood up. "Lead me to it."

"But my mother pays Eric twelve. It's not fair."

"Sure it's fair," Justin said. "He gets a commission and I earn eight dollars. Where's the mower?"

He was so eager to get started that he ignored Allison's fuming. "Eric's such a cheat," she was muttering as she led Justin off to the detached three-car garage.

Suddenly I realized Zeus hadn't followed his master. The dog was lying on his side sleeping. I got up to tiptoe away. He opened one eye and fixed it on me. "Just going to see what they're doing," I told him.

He sat up. Now both eyes were on me. "Nice doggie," I said. But I knew the jig was up. Justin was out of sight. The wolf dog had me at his mercy. I took a step. Zeus stood up. "Help!" I yelled.

Justin and Allison came dashing back from the garage. "What's wrong?" Justin asked.

I was still so shook up about the camping idea that I couldn't think clearly. "You left me alone with this beast," I complained.

Justin grunted. Allison groaned.

"Suki has a wild imagination," she said. "I mean, really. It's amazing what she can come up with."

"I can't believe you're still scared of Zeus," Justin said.

"I'm not," I said.

It was obvious neither of them believed me, and I didn't know how to explain that the fear didn't come from my head. It was a shiver in my blood that my brain couldn't control. Who wanted to be scared? I longed to be brave and calm so they'd respect me— so I could respect myself.

We all went to check out the lawn mower. It was an old power mower that was hard to start, but Justin gave some mighty yanks on the cord and finally roared off with it across the almost-dry lawn.

"Why did you have to do me in like that, Allison?" I asked. "You tricked me into saying I'd go camping, and you know I can't do it."

"Yes, you can, Suki. You'll do it because you like him. You got used to his dog, didn't you?"

"No, I didn't," I said miserably.

"Well, you almost did. Believe me. This'll be good for you."

I didn't believe her, not one bit.

Allison suggested that she and I make lunch while Justin was busy mowing. We went to her old-fashioned, high-ceilinged kitchen, which is so big you walk half a block from the sink to the refrigerator. I decided on lettuce, cheese, and salsa sandwiches while Allison made Toad his usual peanut butter and jelly on toast.

Toad nudged me with his elbow. He wanted me to read him *Hop on Pop*. It was his favorite, but everyone in his family hated it because they'd read it to him so often.

"Not now, Toad. I mean, Tyler," I said.

"So how about we do it this weekend?" Allison asked.

"Camp out?" I listened to the lawn mower growling outside and tried to think. Suddenly I remembered that my father was due home, my darling Daddy-o, the perfect excuse. "Sure, this weekend would be fine," I said as if I meant it.

"Great. Oh, you won't regret this, Suki. It'll be terrific."

I hadn't heard Allison so excited about anything in years. Was it because she was wild about Justin herself? I hoped not. "And what do we do for water and light and stuff like that?" I asked.

"We bring water from the house and use flashlights," Allison explained.

"Oh. Uh-huh. Of course." No need to panic, I told myself. You're not going to do this. They can't make you. But I was so nervous that I overloaded the last sandwich with salsa and dropped it on the floor.

"We'll plan it with Justin as soon as he finishes mowing," Allison said as she wiped up my mess.

"First I better talk to my parents."

"Come on, Suki. It's only my backyard. They won't object."

"They don't know Justin."

"You're looking for an excuse not to do it, aren't you?"

"Me? How can you say such a thing?" I asked in pretend indignation.

"So don't mention Justin to your folks. He can bring Zeus along to protect us. You'll be perfectly safe."

Perfectly safe at night in the woods with Zeus? Yeah, sure. The lawn mower yowled close by the kitchen door. I wondered if it was possible to die of fright.

Chapter 8

$\mathcal{J}$t turned so cool that evening after Dolores and I finished eating our grilled cheese sandwiches and tomato soup that I went up to my bedroom for a sweater. In Mr. Auerbach's backyard, Justin and his father had their long narrow heads together as they worked over an outdoor grill. Mr. Auerbach started laughing at something, a strangled laugh that sounded as if it needed oiling. I hoped that meant they liked each other better and Justin wouldn't have to leave.

The phone was ringing when I got back downstairs. I took Mom's call in the kitchen, where Dolores's thick fingers were delicately peeling a grape. After Mom and I had assured each other we were fine, I asked *her* about hiring Justin.

"Maybe he could paint something," I said. "The back of the garage is peeling."

"Does he have house-painting experience?"

"I don't know. The point is he needs to earn some money."

"Suki, I don't think—"

"Wait." I threw my backup suggestion at her before she could say no. "You always say the garage is useless with all the junk in it. What if I help Justin clear it out?"

"Not until we decide what to throw away."

"Can you get around to it soon?"

"Suki, be reasonable. I'm not sure *when* I'll be home. And after your father gets there, he'll have too much to do to worry about the garage."

She obviously wasn't going to put Justin to work at our house. I was miffed. "You're standing in the way of my first romance, Mom."

"Honey, please, don't give me a hard time long-distance."

"Doesn't my happiness matter to you?" I asked.

"It certainly does, but I can't do much about it until I get home."

"Oh, by the way," I threw in, "Allison has this crazy idea about us camping out in her woods. You won't let me do *that*, will you?"

"You mean in her backyard? Why not? So long as her parents say it's okay and you take proper precautions. Enjoy, sweetheart."

"I can't believe it! How can you let me do something dangerous like camping out in the woods alone? Don't you love me anymore, Mom?"

My mother knows me too well to fall for a question like that. "If you're afraid of doing it, why did you ask me?"

"Mom!" I protested.

"I have to go, Suki," she said. "If you do go camp out, take enough warm clothes. It can get pretty cold at night in June. I love you," she cooed and hung up on me.

Mom hadn't given me a chance to mention that Justin would be with us. She's pretty liberal, but I didn't know how she stood on coed camping. Maybe she'd be against it. That could be my excuse! Except what if I mentioned Justin and his dog, and Mom agreed with Allison that they'd provide extra protection for us. Then what could I say? Unless I just flat out said I didn't want to go. But then Allison and Justin would be alone in the woods together. I'd be practically throwing them into each other's arms.

I groaned and turned to Dolores. "Tell me the truth," I said. "Do you think a boy could ever possibly be attracted to me?"

She popped a grape into her mouth and frowned at me. "Men like to be liked. Sometimes you show you like them, they like you back."

"Well, I mean, am I a *little* pretty?" I coaxed.

She nodded. "Don't worry. You get your man someday."

My oracle! I wondered if she had any Greek blood. I trotted back upstairs to my Olympus shelf with a box of Mom's Thanksgiving dinner candles and lit one for each of the gods there: one for Aphrodite, one for Zeus, one for Hera so she wouldn't get jealous and be mean to me, one for Apollo, and one for Artemis. I even borrowed a roll of postage stamps from my father's desk to represent the messenger god, Hermes. He was supposed to be clever, and I needed somebody clever to help me out of the fix I was in.

For good measure, I set one of my mother's law books up on the shelf so that Athena, goddess of wisdom, wouldn't be slighted. I hadn't bothered to represent the other male gods: Poseidon, who ruled the sea, or Hades, god of the underground, or Hephaestus, the crippled one who made things in his forge, or Dionysus, the god of wine. I figured they couldn't do much for me and hoped they wouldn't mind being ignored. The shelf was getting overcrowded as it was.

While the candles were burning I closed my eyes and clasped my hands, emptying my mind in readiness for any message the gods wanted to send me. Nothing came. But when I opened my eyes again, Hermes' candle had tipped and was dripping hot wax on the stamps. Next thing I knew I'd be burning down the house. I blew out the candle flames and went to the window to check on my neighbors.

I could see a slab of meat on a platter set atop a rickety table next to the grill. Mr. Auerbach was testing the heat of his fire the way my father did, by holding his hand over the coals. Apparently he didn't think they were hot enough because he gestured with his head and he and Justin went back inside the house. Zeus didn't follow them—not allowed in the house, I guessed. The dog stood braced with his head turned over his shoulder, watching until they'd gone.

Then he began acting strangely. He hunkered down and slunk along the ground to the grill, where he stopped and checked the house. Abruptly he lunged for the meat and ran to the back fence below me with it. I could see him holding his stolen dinner in place on the ground with one paw as he ripped pieces off it with his teeth. In seconds he'd gobbled up that whole slab of steak. I had to laugh at the guilty way he looked back at the house.

I was still giggling to myself when Mr. Auerbach returned to the grill carrying a big bowl of something. Justin followed him with a tray. Mr. Auerbach did a double take when he saw the empty platter. Of course, he spotted Zeus, licking his lips by the fence. Boy, could that man yell! You'd have thought he was a wolf himself, the way he howled. He stomped around and shook his fist in a tantrum that Toad couldn't have matched. What a fuss over a piece of meat!

I couldn't believe what I saw next. Justin must have said something his father didn't like because Mr. Auerbach wheeled around suddenly and smacked him across the cheek. My jaw was still hanging open when Zeus came flying through the air and Justin threw himself between his father and his dog just in time.

"Down, boy. Down, Zeus. It's all right," Justin yelled as he wrestled Zeus away from his father. Their voices got too low for me to hear after that. Finally I saw Mr. Auerbach turn on his heel and walk into the house. When his father was gone, Justin folded up like an aluminum lawn chair and let go of Zeus. The dog squatted on his haunches next to Justin, as calm as if there weren't going to be any consequences. But I knew there would be.

I ran downstairs and out the kitchen door past Dolores. When I got to the fence, Justin was still bent over with his head bowed. "I saw what happened," I said.

"Do you spend all your time spying on me?" Justin snapped.

His anger stopped me short. "I'm sorry. I was just getting a sweater up in my room, and I happened to look out the window."

"I'm sorry, too, Suki," he said as if he really was, and he stood up. "My father and I put on quite a show. I can't blame you for watching."

"I could lend you some money for your plane ticket home," I said, because I didn't know what else to offer to make him feel better. "I have most of my allowance in a bank account, and I don't have to buy birthday gifts for anyone until November."

"Thanks," he said. "But I don't want to borrow your money. I told 'Gerard' I'd pay for the steak. He said he didn't care about the meat. Then he said today was his birthday. How was I supposed to know it was his birthday? If I'd known, I'd have gotten him a present. . . . Or made him something."

"You still can," I said.

"I don't want to now. He says I have to get rid of Zeus or get out."

"You're kidding."

"No, he meant it."

"He was probably just upset. Wait until he calms down."

"I made a mistake coming here," Justin said. "I should have stuck it out with Mom and her boyfriend. There's no way I can live with my father."

He sounded so bleak. And what could I do for him? "Justin, come to my house and we'll talk about it," I said.

"I'd have to bring Zeus."

"That's okay," I said. And off I went to tell Dolores we were having company.

To my surprise, she promptly heaved herself from the chair and filled a mixing bowl with water for Zeus. We settled in the kitchen because that seemed the sensible place for the dog, and she heated up the leftover tomato soup for Justin. What's more, when he was sitting there eating it, she asked him if he wanted a grilled cheese sandwich.

"Well, I don't want to bother you," he said.

"No bother." Her cheeks lifted in one of her rare smiles.

"Gracias," he said.

"De nada," Dolores said. I wouldn't have been surprised if next she'd shaken hands with Zeus, who was sitting beside Justin's chair.

I sat down across from Justin at the kitchen table. "You know," I said, "your father must have some feeling about you being his son or he wouldn't have let you come to New York."

"Or else he just wanted to spite my mother. He knew she felt bad that I wanted to leave her."

"You could give him the benefit of the doubt," I said. "He could have wanted to see what you were like. I mean, that's normal, isn't it?"

"Yeah, but whatever he expected wasn't what he got. Besides, *he's* not what I wanted."

"You go back home?" Dolores asked.

"If I can figure out how. My father only sent me a one-way ticket to get here."

"Your mother will pay for you to come home," Dolores said.

Justin shook his head. "She doesn't have any money. And I'm not going to ask her."

"Then how will you get to Colorado?" I asked.

"I don't know." He took a deep breath, and his lips quirked up. "Allison says you've got a great imagination, Suki. Can you figure out how I can earn hundreds of dollars fast, short of robbing a bank?"

"You could sell the dog," Dolores said.

Justin looked shocked. "Never."

89

"If your father gets disgusted enough, he'll *send* you back," I said.

"That should be easy—I mean to get him disgusted. He throws a fit about every little thing—like if I forget to flip the valve back from shower to tub and he gets squirted with cold water by mistake. Or if I track mud on the kitchen floor. He even gets mad if I walk around barefooted. And yesterday he caught me with my feet on his crummy coffee table and he says, 'I guess it's no surprise that you don't know how to behave in a house. Your mother never was much of a housekeeper.' I almost socked him then."

"You can cook?" Dolores asked.

"Yeah, but nothing fancy."

"Make him supper after work. You are too young to fight your father and win."

Justin took a while to think over her advice. "Maybe," he said finally. "I guess it *was* his birthday. And Zeus did eat his steak. And I did mouth off to him again."

Meanwhile, Dolores was offering Zeus a chunk of cheese. I held my breath as he took it politely from the ends of her fingers. He wagged his tail and she petted him roughly. Was I the only one in the world afraid of dogs?

Justin and I went into the study to see what was on TV. Zeus followed us. "Nice lady," Justin said to me.

"Dolores?" I thought about it. "Umm," I admitted.

She wasn't Mrs. Esposito, but Dolores did have her good points.

I stretched my hand out to pet Zeus and felt hurt when he coiled himself up out of my reach against Justin's leg.

"What happened to make you so scared of dogs?" Justin asked.

"Oh, nothing much. One bit me when I was little." I'd been afraid of dogs before that just on principle because they had teeth and barked. But being bitten made a better excuse.

Not for Justin, though. "I got bitten by a snake when I was six, and nearly died," he said. "It didn't make me scared of snakes."

"No? Why not? What's wrong with *you*?"

He laughed. "I guess you're just supersensitive," he said.

"I am not. I'm scared of a lot of things because I'm smart enough to know you can get hurt."

"Well, that's one way to look at it," he said. "Let's talk about the camp-out."

"Will you stay in Allison's woods until you can figure out a way to get home?"

"Zeus and I may have no choice if my father kicks us out."

I gulped. "I guess we could help get you set up and then keep you supplied with what you need for as long as you need it. I mean, I don't mind bringing food and stuff all through the summer if I have to."

"Thanks, Suki. I really appreciate that offer. And I'm looking forward to having you and Allison keep me company the first night."

He was still expecting me to stay with him! How had I gotten into this? "But what if it rains again?" I said desperately.

"It won't."

I raised an eyebrow as if I doubted him. "Well, we'll see."

What I'd better do was beg Zeus—the god, not the dog—for the worst storm of the century, one that would last all summer. Or maybe I could apply to someone to get my father to come home a day sooner. If Dad arrived tomorrow instead of Saturday, Justin and Allison would have to sleep out in the woods without me because I should be with Dad on his first evening home. In fact, he might need me around for the whole summer. I'd surely be able to convince him of that.

It wasn't until I was lying in bed that night that it occurred to me I was going to miss a lot if I got out of the camp-out. Being fearful was a drag. It kept me from doing so many things other people enjoyed. Instead of little favors, what I should be asking my Greek gods for was courage. That would improve my whole life. I'd always thought courage was some-thing you were born with or without, but what if you could acquire it? What if I made myself go camping with them and faced my fear the way Allison was always telling me I should? Would I wind up braver?

My heart thumped solemnly while I considered the question. The trouble was, the only way to find out for sure was to try it, and I didn't know if I could make myself do that.

Chapter 9

The paperback historical romance that Allison had given me for my birthday kept me up reading so late that I was still asleep at ten Friday morning when Allison called. "Come on over," she said. "Justin's here."

"He is? How come?" I was dismayed that he had gone to see her instead of me.

"Just come." Allison sounded impatient, and I was anxious not to leave her alone with Justin, so instead of pushing for information, I hung up and hurried.

My slimming shorts were in the wash. Instead I put on my flowered shorts, which are cute but not figure-flattering. I did find a blue T-shirt. Boys always come out liking blue in those girls' magazine surveys.

Dolores was in the yard in shimmery morning sunlight, slowly wiping off the outdoor furniture. I was surprised to see her out of the kitchen and actually cleaning something. Maybe she felt she'd rested up long enough from taking care of her father. Anyway, I took a bran muffin from the freezer, yelled to Dolores that I was going to Allison's, and sped off on my bike. I ate the frozen muffin as I rode. It tasted fine, but halfway there my legs began to ache from pumping so hard and my stomach didn't feel so good, either.

When I finally reached Allison's driveway, something whipped by my knee and then a hairy monster rounded the corner of the house and charged right at me. "Aaaaagh!" I screamed and went down with my bike. Zeus was on me instantly, ready to rip out my throat or my cheek or some other critical body part. I did what any sensible person does in the face of danger. I fainted. Well, it might not have been a real faint. Whatever it was, when I opened my eyes, Zeus was licking my face and Allison and Justin were peering down at me critically.

"Are you okay?" Justin asked.

I wasn't sure yet. "Uh," I said, trying to fend off his dog. Justin grabbed Zeus by the scruff of his neck and hoisted him off me.

"What happened?" Allison asked.

"He attacked me." I pointed at Zeus. Foolishly. I mean, if they'd given me a second to think—but they didn't.

In fact, they started laughing. They cackled and

giggled and chuckled while I sat up and took stock of myself. I'd scraped my knee, but otherwise I didn't seem to be wounded. Zeus wanted to lick my knee. I jerked it away from him.

"Suki, he was just glad to see you. He likes you," Justin assured me in the patient way you repeat something to babies.

"Well, I don't like him back." It wasn't the smartest thing to say to a boy who loved his dog, but I was still shook up. Justin stiffened. Fine, great, what a big help you are, I told my Olympic deities silently. Now Justin really hates me. I felt like crying, but that would only make matters worse, so instead I stood up.

Allison retrieved a Frisbee. *That* was what had sailed by my knee and what Zeus had been chasing. "The front wheel on your bike is bent," Allison said. "You better leave it here for one of my brothers to fix."

"Fine," I said. Her brothers had fixed my bike before. They liked to do it because I baked stuff for them in exchange. "So," I said as if I were my normal, cheerful self, "what are you guys up to?"

"We were waiting for you to come so we could plan the camp-out," Allison said.

I kept smiling. Having disgraced myself with the dog, I wasn't about to remind Allison that I'd never slept anywhere but in my own bed except when I went on vacation with my parents, or occasionally when I'd stayed over at her house. And the first time

I ever did that, I got so homesick my father had had to come and get me in the middle of the night. "So when's the great camp-out to be?" I asked.

"Tonight, after dinner," Justin said. "But we'll set up the tent and put the stuff in it this afternoon. You won't mind Zeus being with us, will you, Suki?" Justin asked.

"Uh-uh," I said. I even managed to lean past Justin and gingerly pat Zeus's back where the hair was too thick for him to notice.

"Camping out will be a good experience for you," Allison said.

"She's not scared of that, too?" Justin sounded disbelieving.

"Of course I'm not." I glared at Allison to keep her from totaling my reputation altogether. "Come on, now. Stop beating on me and let's plan this thing. . . . I'll bring the food. We can start with just enough for a day, right?"

"At least," Allison said. "We'll use my brother's big tent. It'll sleep four. We'd better make a list of what else we'll need." Eagerly, she led the way to her backyard, where she had a clipboard and pen waiting on the redwood table. I followed, struck cold by a terror I couldn't control.

After dinner, Justin had said. Fine, then if I needed to chicken out on this thing, my father could get back unexpectedly this evening. I'd announce his arrival to Allison around dinnertime and say I couldn't possibly leave him alone on his first evening home in a week. I'd better talk Dolores into lying for me in case Allison checked to find out if he was really there. Dolores would back me up. I was sure she would. Thinking that, I relaxed a little.

Allison loves organizing things. Call a committee and she's the first to volunteer for it. Me, I slink out of sight. I don't mind doing the posters or writing publicity. I just hate sitting around and chewing over boring details with people who never do anything but bicker.

"Where's Toad?" I asked.

"Ball game with Pete." Pete was Eric's twin brother.

While Allison and Justin made lists of what we needed and who was responsible for what, I made eye contact with Zeus. That dog reminded me of one of those gods who'd do you good or dirt on a whim. Not that his amber eyes had a mean look, but his ears stuck up in a pointy, wolfish way and his tongue hung out as long as the tongue on Little Red Riding Hood's wolf. And why did he have to have black lips? Of course, he was a dog. He'd probably look strange with soft pink ones. But why was he staring back at me?

His tail was certainly handsome, the way it feathered out, and his blunt black nose was kind of cute in a squooshy sort of way. It twitched. I wondered if that meant something critical. Was he thinking how tasty my plump flesh would be? I shuddered. Petting him was one thing. Sleeping with him was another. And Justin would probably insist on having him inside the tent. Don't worry, I told myself. Zeus could have the sleeping bag assigned to me while I slept safely in my own bed.

"Suki."

"What?" I jumped at the sound of Allison's voice.

"Can you bake some cookies fast? I've got cheese and bread for lunch. Breakfast can just be cereal."

"I told you, I'll bring the food. You bring the equipment."

"Yeah, well, we need to know if you're bringing stuff that needs to be cooked," Justin said.

"How about turkey dogs and hot sauce for dinner tomorrow night and everything else cold?"

"Sounds good to me," Justin said. "I hope we're pitching the tent where it can't be seen." He looked at Allison. "Just in case I burn the dinner for my father tonight and he decides to come looking for me again."

"You're cooking dinner for him?" I asked.

"Right. It was Dolores's idea, remember? If it doesn't work, I'm out of there for good."

"Don't worry," Allison said. "Our woods are really dense." We all looked at the rumpled wall of green bushes and trees that blocked the view of the river and the bike path. It seemed miles away, past the mowed backyard lawn and the field of thistles and blackberry bushes and daisies. "This spot is hidden from everything. Nobody could find us unless they knew where to look," Allison said.

Immediately I imagined somebody sneaking up

on us in a canoe while we slept and kidnapping one or all of us. My heart jumped just thinking about it.

Later, to my delight, Justin walked home with me while Zeus trotted beside us. That is, I was delighted until Justin started talking.

"Allison's got it made, doesn't she?" he said. "She has *everything*."

"Yes, she's pretty lucky." I was thinking of the big family that she complained about but that I envied her for.

"I bet she's popular too, huh?" Justin couldn't stop wallowing in praise of his goddess.

"I guess," I said. "If you mean people vote for her to do things. Like she's been class president and captain of a volleyball team."

Why had I picked Miss Perfect for best friend, I was asking myself, when Justin said, "I wish I was like that."

"Aren't you?" I asked him.

"Me? No. When I went to public school—that's when we lived in Wyoming—I had one friend, and he was an Indian."

"So? What's wrong with being an Indian?"

"Nothing, except he went back to the reservation every weekend, so I never saw him except in school. We had some pretty good talks during lunch, though— you know, about life and what's the point of it when you're going to die anyway—that kind of stuff."

"Really?" I was impressed. "My father's the only

one I can talk big issues with. My mother's more interested in personal things." Like why didn't I make other friends besides Allison. My mother's concern was that Allison might move away or get interested in some boy and drop me. She wanted me to have a backup friend so that I wouldn't fall into a black hole of despair if I lost Allison someday.

"Your father must be a neat guy." The wistful way Justin said that reminded me of his father, and I felt terrible for him.

"Allison's not much for philosophy," I said, to undermine his image of her. "She doesn't believe in wasting time thinking."

"She's probably right. . . . It's funny you two are such good friends when you're so different."

That stung me. "Well, I have some good qualities," I said.

"You do?" He was grinning. "Name one."

"I'm loyal." I winced because my recent description of Allison had been disloyal.

"Like Zeus," Justin said. "Right. So how come you're scared of everything, Suki?"

I considered making up a story about a tortured early childhood, but I liked him so much that I had to be honest. "I'm just a natural-born coward," I admitted. "I don't want to be, though."

"Of course you don't," he said with sympathy. "Here." He handed me Zeus's leash. "Go ahead and walk him to your house. I'll meet you there."

101

"What?"

"Go ahead." He waved me on. "Just take him home with you. I'll come pick him up after I do the food shopping for tonight."

I looked at him: straight nose, narrow eyes, firm mouth. He meant it. He expected me to walk off alone with his wolf dog while he went to the supermarket. "Uhgg," I said, strangling on objections.

He put the leash in my fingers, closed them around it, and began to run down the road. He had more than two miles to go.

"Justin!" I screamed.

He was already a doll-sized figure down the road. "What?"

"How about I do the shopping for you?" I was thinking I could get Dolores to drive me.

"Walk the dog, Suki."

I looked at Zeus. He looked back at me. I didn't have a clue as to what he was thinking. I gulped. Well, what could I do? I'd already humiliated myself enough for one day. Besides, I can admit to cowardice, and maybe Justin thinks I'm exaggerating. But if I actually demonstrate it, he'll despise me. I took two steps toward home on wobbly legs. Zeus waited on a slack leash looking bored.

"So," I said in my most honeyed tone, "you want to go for a walk with me, Zeusy-woosy?"

He didn't answer. The strong silent type. Even *people* like that scare me. Gingerly I began tiptoeing down Rosendale. Not actually tiptoeing, but I was so nervous, it came close. Zeus followed me as if he'd been doing it his whole life.

"Boy, are you well trained," I told him when I finally collapsed on my own front steps with the leash still in my hand. I stiffened some when I realized I'd put my nose within easy snap of Zeus's teeth. But rather than taking advantage of the situation, he flopped down next to me, so close my leg touched his. I unclenched my fingers from his leash and patted his back. "Good boy," I said. "You're a very good boy." I meant it, too.

We both sat waiting for Justin. My Apollo! But what good did it do me to adore him with Allison around for competition? The noble thing would be to give Justin up, ignore my embarrassing jealousy, and leave them to each other.

✳✳✳

"So how did it go?" Justin asked when he finally showed up about an hour later.

"Fine," I said. Zeus stood up, wagging his tail at his master.

"See how easy it is?" Justin said.

"A cinch," I said and ignored the image still stuck in my head of Zeus going for Mr. Auerbach as if he'd like to kill him. Justin took Zeus and his grocery bag home. I should have asked him what he was making his father for dinner. And what had he used for money? The eight dollars he'd gotten for the lawn mowing? Or probably he had a little money with him, just not enough for a plane ticket.

I retreated to my room to rest from the morning's ordeal. Tears came to my eyes as I passed my dresser mirror and saw the dirt smudges on my face and my curls going every which way like broken bedsprings. "O Aphrodite," I murmured, "if you could only make me beautiful, I'd be your slave forever."

Hopeless, I thought, looking at my mirror image. Even Aphrodite wasn't that powerful. Besides, what I needed more than beauty right now was courage. Those Greek gods were big on courage. They'd faced monsters of the deep and giants on land and been tormented and tortured and fought legendary battles. They'd aided heroes in accomplishing deeds of valor and daring. Maybe they could make me brave enough to spend a night in the woods in a tent with my best friend and the boy I loved. They had to be good for granting something or people wouldn't have worshiped them as long as they did.

"O Apollo, O Hera, and Aphrodite and Artemis and all of you," I began. "Help me not to be so scared. And if you can't manage that, help me to pretend not to be so scared. Please!"

Chapter 10

$\mathcal{A}$llison called just as I put my peanut butter cookies into the oven. "Bad news," she said. Her grandparents and a bachelor uncle were passing through town, and her mother had invited them to stay overnight. "Mom wants me to help entertain them and to keep Toad out of trouble. You and Justin can camp out without me. I'll check in with you tomorrow sometime."

"Oh, no, that's okay, Allison. I wouldn't go without you," I said hastily. "I'll wait until tomorrow, too." And to myself I said, thank you, Aphrodite. Thank you, Zeus. Or whoever. Tomorrow my father would be home, and I wouldn't even have to lie about his arrival.

Cheerfully, I called Justin to relay the news.

"Yeah, well, let's see how the dinner goes," he said. "Maybe I won't need to move out tonight and we can all wait until tomorrow."

"Well, should I lug the food over to Allison's or not? I mean, do you want to bother setting up camp?"

"Tomorrow's soon enough. We'll have all day to get the campsite in order, and that'll be better than fumbling around in the dark."

"Fine," I said cheerfully. "I'll call Allison." I sashayed over to the oven to check on my cookies and set them out on the counter to cool. I was doing a high kick followed by a pirouette because I felt so good when the phone rang again.

"Honey, I hate to do this," Dad said, "but I'm going to have to stay another day. Turns out tomorrow's the only time the committee could get together to plan next year's conference. You can hang in there with Dolores until Sunday, can't you?"

"Daddy, I miss you!" I wailed.

"I miss you, too, sweetheart. Believe me, I can't wait to get home."

"Well," I warned him, "if you don't come home tomorrow, I might go camping out in the woods with Allison and the boy next door."

"A boy? This boy you're interested in?" Dad sounded properly alarmed. "How old is he?"

"My age," I said airily, knowing I had him. "Don't worry. He's a nice kid and he's not interested in me. Allison's the one he likes."

"And you're camping in the woods with both of them? Where?"

"In the back of Allison's property." As soon as I

said it, I realized my mistake, but it was too late.

"Oh. Well," Dad said, "if you do it, be sure to take a flashlight. I presume Allison's folks will be home?"

"Sure, they'll be home. But Dad, I don't want to do it."

"Why, Suki? The experience might be good for you. I'm glad you're willing to try it."

"What?" I gasped. All my life my father has been trying to protect me from every possible physical harm. Mom says he was so worried that something might happen to me that he didn't take me to a playground until I was five. As for bike riding, I was finally allowed to ride in the road only because I told him Allison wouldn't be my friend unless I could go where she went, and he knew I couldn't live without Allison.

"You think it's great for me to risk being bitten by a snake or attacked by some maniac roaming the woods, Dad?" I asked.

"Suki, if you're that upset about my staying an extra day, I'll come home." He sounded concerned, as if something might be wrong that I wasn't telling him. But nothing was wrong. I was just scared. As usual. Suddenly I was embarrassed.

"It's okay, Dad. You can stay for your meeting," I said nobly.

"Don't go camping if you don't want to," he said. "I mean, if you're afraid—"

"I'm not," I lied. "I was just putting you on. After all, what's there to be scared about?"

I waited hopefully for him to think of something. He was a pro at imagining the worst. But all he said was, "I know you're maturing, becoming independent. Your mother keeps telling me. Someday you'll learn to drive. You'll leave us and go off to college, and I'll have to get used to it." He sounded so resigned, I felt as if I was being pushed out into the world that instant. "I'm not ready," I wanted to yell.

"Daddy, I'm only in middle school," I murmured. "Maybe you *should* come home."

"No, no. You're right. I trust you. Have fun with your friends. Just be careful." He sounded as if he were making a big sacrifice to let me go. "Say no, Daddy. Forbid me to go," I was about to yell, but he was telling me how much he loved me and how important I was to him. My brain whirled. Somehow the conversation had gotten away from me.

After Dad hung up, I brooded. So much for being an overprotected only child. I stomped out of the kitchen and upstairs, straight to my Olympus shelf, and let them have it.

"Now I know why you stopped being worshiped," I told them. "You lost it, didn't you? I should have guessed you don't have any pull or push or power. Whatever. I asked you for courage, and you didn't give me that. But at least you could have gotten my father home on time."

I found a container for the peanut butter cookies and stowed them with the other stuff I'd started collecting for the camp-out. Then I called Allison to tell her we weren't setting up camp until tomorrow. "Good," she said. "Mom's got me picking up the whole house to get ready for the relatives, and I can't just shove things in closets, either. Grandma opens them to check up on us. See you tomorrow, Suki."

The afternoon was over anyway, I thought, as I put down the phone. Justin was probably already busy preparing dinner for his father. I wished he'd asked me to help him, but he hadn't. Should I call him up and offer assistance? Probably not. Chances were he'd feel better doing it himself. And where was Zeus? In with his master until Mr. Auerbach got home and kicked him out, I supposed.

I leaned out the window and noticed my beloved stuffed tiger still lying in the bush. Sacrificed for nothing. Well, tomorrow I'd give Tiger a proper burial and get on with life. No more talking to gods and goddesses from the long-dead past. I'd clear them off my shelf and go back to Unitarianism. At least it was a modern, sensible religion and it satisfied my parents.

***

When Dolores finally got back from the supermarket and started cooking our supper, I put aside the book I was reading and went down to see what smelled so good.

"Why you look sad?" she asked me.

"Dad's not coming home until Sunday, and I miss everybody."

She stopped stirring and covered the pot. "He call me, too," she said. "Come. I tell your fortune."

"You're a fortune-teller?"

"Sit down," Dolores said.

I sat, shivering in excitement, while she went off to her room. In a minute she returned with a deck of ordinary-looking playing cards with ducks on the back. Somehow it didn't surprise me to find out that Dolores had the power to foresee the future. It was easy to imagine her intoning revelations through some oracle hole in an old Greek temple.

She started laying the cards out on the table opposite me in what looked suspiciously like a game of solitaire. Except her eyes were fixed inward on messages from the beyond. Or did that only happen at séances? Anyway, I leaned my cheeks on my fists and waited.

"What do you want to know?" she asked me.

"Will Justin ever like me?"

She laid out more cards. The pattern sure looked like solitaire. Could she really tell fortunes or was she faking it? Before I could decide, she tapped a thick finger on a jack of clubs that she'd just put on a red ten. "This means 'Yes.'"

"Really? How soon? I mean this year, this summer, tomorrow?"

She turned over more cards and studied the situation. I was about to suggest she put the king of spades on the queen of hearts when she spoke.

"Soon. This summer."

"You're kidding! Where do you read that?"

She pursed her lips, tapping a finger on the ace. Then rapidly she began turning cards again. *"But!"* she said with such force I nearly jumped out of my seat. I wasn't the only dramatic person in the house.

"But what?"

"But you have to overcome first."

"What?" I squawked. "What do I have to overcome?"

She shrugged. "The cards don't say." She pointed to the queen of hearts. "That is you," she said. "See? She is top of the pile."

"Wow!" I was impressed at being tops.

Satisfied with my reaction, Dolores folded the cards together and stood up. "Now we eat dinner," she said. "You like chili?"

"Sure."

Her chili was so peppery I could barely eat it, but I told her it was delicious because her fortune-telling had come out well for me.

"I made it by recipe," she said proudly. She showed me the recipe, which was from an article entitled "Hot Stuff from the Far West." It came out of one of the girls' magazines I've been reading to learn how to appeal to boys. "I like to cook," Dolores said. "Maybe I take lessons."

"Good idea, Dolores." I wondered what other ideas she'd get from those magazines as I helped her clear away the dinner dishes.

The doorbell rang. I opened up, and there was Justin with Zeus. "How did dinner go?" I asked.

"Bad. Can I come in?"

I stepped aside, and Justin walked into the entry hall, followed by Zeus. "Kitchen?" Justin asked.

"No, let's go up to my room." I was thinking it would be cozier without Dolores being part of the conversation, but I left my door open in case she felt the need to check on me and my male caller. Mrs. Esposito would have, but Dolores treated me more like an adult, which I was beginning to like.

Zeus made himself at home on the shaggy rug beside my bed and fixed his eyes on his master.

Outside my bedroom window the sky was pale green, and even though the sun wouldn't be going down for another couple of hours, the leafy trees were making their own dark. Justin stared down into his father's backyard as he balanced one knee on my window seat. I hoped he wasn't going to ask me about the Olympus shelf. It would be embarrassing to admit that I'd been taking the ancient Greek gods seriously.

Justin kept staring into the yard without saying anything.

"So what happened?" I asked.

"We got into it again," he answered.

I sat down on my bed close to the window seat Justin had claimed. Zeus shifted his head to my foot. I flinched, and then melted. My good buddy dog!

Waiting for Justin to unload his trouble, I felt like poor Calypso, who had wooed Odysseus for seven years while he was stuck on her island. She never did get him to stop gazing out to sea toward his wife and his native land. I mean, it's frustrating to be with the one you love when he's yearning for someone else.

Suddenly Justin turned around and I stopped thinking about myself. He looked as if he was full of tears but couldn't cry.

"You better tell me what happened," I said, absently rubbing Zeus behind the ears.

"I cooked meatballs and spaghetti," Justin began. "I made the sauce from canned tomatoes and onions and garlic the way my mom makes it, but he said he's allergic to garlic. He put cold canned beans on his spaghetti and sprinkled cheese on top instead. I must have made a face because he tried to make me taste it, and we got into a big argument, which came down to his saying that I don't respect him. 'You think your mother's always right?' he asks me. 'You think the divorce was my fault?'

"I told him yeah, I did. Then he exploded. The things he said—I hate him now. He may be smart about computers, but he's a jerk about my mother.

113

And I told him that. I told him he was a real . . ."
Justin swallowed and fell silent.

Then he continued, "Well, I lost my temper and said stuff I shouldn't have. So to get back at me, he reminded me about getting rid of my dog. I told him not to worry, he wouldn't have to put up with Zeus *or* me."

"What did he say to that?"

"That I could do as I pleased. What I did was write and tell my mother I need to come home. She's going to have to borrow the money, probably from the guy she's with. But—meanwhile I'll camp out in the woods like we planned until Mom sends me a train or plane ticket. I used your address in the letter, Suki. I hope that's okay?"

"Oh, sure."

He nodded, said thanks, and went back to staring out the window although the dark was rising up so fast there wasn't much to see.

"You can stay here tonight," I said. "There's a couch in Dad's office. You'll just have to be careful not to disturb his piles of papers." I thought of the magazines and books stacked on the couch. I'd have to move those. I could put him in my parents' bedroom, but Mom had her office space in there and that was even more untouchable.

"I don't know. I guess I could do that," Justin said. "But I've got to go back and get my duffle bag. I want to be completely out of his life."

"It's too bad," I said, feeling sorry for both of us because Justin was going to be out of my life, too.

"I think my mother knew it wouldn't work," Justin said. He was still looking out the window and talking into the dark. "She warned me that he was used to living alone. She said I should be prepared to give him more chances than I thought he deserved—that maybe he was capable of loving a son, but he'd need practice."

"Would you forgive your father if he apologized?"

"He'll never apologize. He's too sure he's right."

I thought of the times I'd gone to sleep in despair and woke up in the morning to find there were possibilities after all. "Maybe tomorrow—" I began.

"No," Justin said. "It's over."

To comfort him, I said, "Anyway, you've got a good mother, Justin."

"The best. Everybody loves my mother, everybody but him." His eyes went back to the window.

"Are you watching for something?" I asked.

"Yeah, he's going to a gun show tonight. I was going with him until we had the fight."

"You mean you like guns?" I asked in dismay.

Justin shrugged. "I hunt some. I've got my own shotgun back home."

Clunk! My Apollo had flaws. I wondered how many little animals he'd killed and decided I'd better not ask because I wasn't going to like the answer. He had enough trouble without having to argue animal

115

rights with me. "You're waiting until he leaves the house to go back for your bag?"

"You got it. No sense tangling with him until he cools down."

"Want to play a game while you're waiting?"

He smiled at me. "What kind?"

I teased him, wide-eyed. "Well, I still have my old Candyland."

"How about Scrabble?"

It turned out Justin was as good a Scrabble player as I am. I won, but not by much, and it was only because I made a seven-letter word and got fifty extra points for using all my letters.

We were going to start another game when he said, "Hey, the lights are out. I'd better get over there now."

I followed him to the back door. Dolores had gone to bed. She'd left the light on over the sink, but otherwise the house was dark. I stood at the back door watching Justin and Zeus cross his yard. What was it about that boy that tied me into knots? Other boys had broader shoulders, and mouths as wide and sensitive. Maybe it was a chemical attraction, or he had an aura I couldn't see that drew me to him. Whatever it was, he took my heart with him as he slipped into his house.

Chapter 11

$\mathcal{J}$ waited a long time. Justin was taking forever to pick up one duffle bag. Unless he'd unpacked it and had to repack it. But he couldn't be a fussy packer with a duffle bag, could he? The lights in Mr. Auerbach's house went off, then came on again. A dog barked. I heard a shout, and suddenly figures tumbled out the back door.

A floodlight threw a cone of light toward me across the dark yard. Justin and Zeus ran through the brightness to where it faded out under the tree. A minute later, Mr. Auerbach walked out the back door with a rifle in his hands. Justin froze. His father marched up to him and thrust the rifle at him with both hands as if he wanted Justin to take it.

"No way!" I heard Justin scream.

Whatever Mr. Auerbach was saying was low-voiced. He put the rifle down, rolled up a sleeve of his shirt, and held his arm out for Justin to see.

Justin turned his head away. "Your own fault," he said loudly. "Why didn't you turn the lights on when you came back for your ticket?"

Mr. Auerbach bent to pick up the rifle and Zeus leaped. Justin threw himself between his dog and his father. I didn't wait to see more. Instead I raced downstairs, barefooted and still in my shorts, rushed through the kitchen, and dashed around the side of our house to the fence. Just as I reached it an object sailed over my head—the branch of a tree?

No, the rifle. I heard it crash against something hard and followed my ears to where it lay against the rocks piled up for our someday rock garden. I picked up the weapon and scooted back indoors. It was heavy and ugly and I hated touching it, but without it they couldn't shoot each other or Zeus, at least.

My hands began to shake. What was I going to do with the thing? I had to get rid of it, stick it where no one would find it. Where? The basement. I flipped on the light at the top of the stairs and toted the rifle down to our dank, unfinished basement where the washer and dryer and storage boxes were the only furnishings besides the furnace and water tanks.

Someone was pounding on our kitchen door. I stood there transfixed as if I were the one in the cone of light and Mr. Auerbach were after me. What I needed to find was a good hiding place for the gun, but I couldn't decide. Finally, I just shoved the rifle behind the furnace. Then I ran back upstairs, turned off the light, and shut the basement door. I stood there listening to my thumping heart and the hum of the refrigerator thinking, there, I'd done it.

But now the front doorbell rang. I didn't have to answer, did I? It was the middle of the night. Suppose it was Justin, though? I crept to the door. "Who is it?"

"Open up." A man's voice. Mr. Auerbach.

I wrung my hands. "I can't," I said. "My parents don't let me open the door to strangers at night." My voice sounded like a scared little kid's. Well, I was a kid and I was scared. Why didn't Dolores wake up? She should be handling this.

"I'm your neighbor and you have something of mine," Mr. Auerbach said.

"No, I don't."

"I saw you, girl." His voice was calm.

"Where's Justin?" I asked.

"He's run off. Don't worry. I'm not going to shoot him. Or his dog. I just want my rifle back."

I whimpered and chewed on my thumb knuckle. Should I call the police? But what could I say? I *had* taken his gun.

Instead, I tiptoed up the bedroom stairs with my hands over my ears. If I didn't answer him, he'd be mad at me. But I didn't know what else to do, except to give him back his gun, and I wasn't about to do that.

At the top step I took my hands off my ears. I

could hear Mr. Auerbach pounding at the kitchen door now. What if he broke it down? Dolores's bedroom was along a hallway from the kitchen. Surely she'd heard all the noise. Unless she was dead. Unless . . . My mind kept tumbling out crazier and crazier notions. Maybe Dolores wasn't in the house at all. Maybe she had snuck off and left me alone. . . .

Suddenly the pounding stopped. Silence for a while. I hoped Mr. Auerbach had gone away. He could have left to call the police, of course. After all, I'd stolen his gun. I crept into my bedroom, closed the door behind me, locked it, and hid under the hand-stitched quilt that had come down to me from my grandmother. I wanted my parents home. I wanted Mrs. Esposito there to defend me. I wanted to know why Dolores hadn't awakened during all that racket. Unless she was as scared as I was.

It wasn't cold but I was shaking. For a while I waited for Justin to ring the bell and claim the asylum I'd offered him. Where had he gone, anyway? Not back into his father's house, certainly. The last thing I remember thinking before sleep claimed me was that I hoped Justin's mother would send him a plane ticket to go home before anything terrible happened.

Chapter 12

$\mathcal{J}$ followed the scent of cinnamon down to the kitchen the next morning and was relieved to see Dolores's bulky figure by the stove. "Did you hear anything last night?" I asked her.

"Hear what?" She flipped the golden toast in the pan. French toast! I was surprised she even knew what that was, but life felt more normal to have her making it.

I replayed my part in the gun scene, only exaggerating a little, and Dolores's eyes widened. She'd fallen asleep with her Walkman plugged into her ears and hadn't heard anything, she said. "Don't worry," she added. "That man comes here, I protect you next time."

I was glad to hear it.

"Where you hide his gun?" she asked me.

"You won't give it back to him?"

She drew herself up in insult. "What kind of question you ask me?"

121

My pal, Dolores! How could I have doubted her? "It's behind the furnace in the basement."

"Bueno," she said. "We leave it there."

Her French toast was creamy on the inside and crispy on the outside with just the right amount of sugar and cinnamon. I raved. Her smile transformed her from a fierce Mayan god to a plump-cheeked Madonna.

I wanted to know what had happened to Justin after I hid the gun but didn't dare go near his house or call there. The only thing I could think to do was go up to my bedroom and call Allison.

As soon as I began telling her about last night, she cut me short. "Suki, I know all about it. Justin's here. He's helping my brother paint the basement right now."

She knew all about it? But this was *my* drama. I'd had a starring role. And then the rest of what she had said struck me. "Justin's there? Why didn't you call me to come over?" I demanded.

"I didn't think you'd be up yet. Anyway, can you believe what a crook Eric is? He's barely paying anything, and Justin's doing half the job. But I can't convince him to be mad about it."

"I could come and watch," I said glumly.

"They're almost finished. What you could do is collect some more food. Stuff that doesn't need refrigeration. Justin's moving into the woods as soon as he finishes painting."

Before I could ask her what he had said about last night, she hung up on me. That Allison! Of course, part of my pique was jealousy that Justin had gone to her instead of to me. Stop being so self-centered, I told myself. Justin's in trouble, and if I really cared about him, I'd be glad to serve him even though he prefers Allison to me.

But I was hurt. Hiding the rifle might not seem like a big deal to either him or Allison, but I was amazed that I'd done it. True, I had acted without thinking, and maybe if I'd thought about it, I wouldn't have done it. But I did do it. I mean, I'd been heroic. And heroes deserve appreciation.

Dutifully, I raided our well-stocked kitchen pantry again. I packed two more shopping bags full of food—tuna fish, beans, pineapple tidbits, peanut butter, jelly, bread and frozen bagels, canned juice, yesterday's home-baked cookies, a can of anchovies, and a big box of sugary cereal. Hefting the four bags, I realized I'd packed to the max I could tote.

"I'm off to Allison's house," I told Dolores, who was playing solitaire at the kitchen table.

"What she need all that food for?"

"It's for Justin. He's camping out to hide from his father."

"And you go camping with him?"

"Me? No way." I'd had all the excitement I could stand last night. "I'm no camper. Believe me, Dolores, I'll be sleeping in my own bed tonight." If my father's arrival wasn't excuse enough, I'd get sick. Bad stomachache. I could groan and bend double if I had to.

"To sleep under the stars is good," Dolores said cryptically as she turned over a card.

Halfway to Allison's house, I was still puzzling over whether the "stars" remark was Dolores's recommendation or an offhand comment. She'd certainly become my Delphic oracle, down to the cryptic messages.

I set the shopping bags down in the road to rest and wished I'd used the wheelbarrow to cart them because my arms felt as if I'd been stretched on a medieval torture rack. My solution was to move the bags along the road, two at a time, in a sort of relay race, or more like a relay crawl. The operation with the bags got me some curious glances from people in passing cars.

Zeus barked when he spotted me trudging up Allison's driveway. He bounded up to me, wagging his tail in a friendly way, but then he licked my face and somehow my shopping bags and I all fell down. Oh, well, I told myself as I sprawled on Allison's driveway with cans rolling away in all directions, at least somebody loves me.

"There you are," Allison said. She and Justin had come around the corner of the house, loaded down with camping gear. Besides his duffle bag, Justin had the tent and Allison had sleeping bags and a pot and a pan, plus a huge backpack. "What happened to you, Suki?"

"Nothing. I've made a conquest. Zeus just greeted me too passionately," I said from my prone position.

They put their stuff down to retrieve my cans from under the bushes and off the lawn. "You're setting up camp this minute?" I asked.

"My father goes in to work mornings on Saturday," Justin said. "Soon as he gets back and realizes I'm gone, he'll check your house. Dolores will probably tell him where you've gone and then—"

"Dolores won't tell," I assured him.

"Well, anyway," Justin persisted, "I want to get going."

"Nobody knows this camping spot but my brothers and me," Allison told him. "I bet even my folks wouldn't be able to find you."

I needed to rest my stressed-out arm muscles—or the stressed-out places where muscles should be. "Can we use a wheelbarrow for this stuff?" I asked. "It's heavy."

Allison reloaded herself and went to the detached, three-car garage for a wheelbarrow. Justin picked up his gear, and I groaned softly to myself as I lifted my plastic bags again. Justin must have heard the groan. "Want me to carry them for you?" he asked.

I didn't see how he could carry any more. "I'm fine," I assured him, but I barely managed to stagger to the garage.

"I thought you had to look after Toad," I said to

Allison when she'd loaded my foodstuffs in the wheelbarrow.

"I was, but my folks took him to the emergency room for stitches after he fell off his tricycle and split his lip. The grandparents went, too."

It was Toad's third visit to the emergency room this year. No doubt they greeted him by name there.

Allison handed off the wheelbarrow to me and led the way across the lawn into the bumpy field full of blackberry bushes and thistles and rocks. The field separated her house from the fringe of woods along the bike path that hid the river from view.

"Okay, Justin," I said. "Give. What was your father so angry about last night?"

"Zeus grabbed his arm to keep him from hitting me."

"Did Zeus bite him?" I asked, nearly emptying the wheelbarrow on a rock.

"No, but he left teeth marks. It was all over nothing again. Just a Chinese lamp identical to one Mom has that she inherited from her mother. I guess the lamps were a pair. Anyway, I asked my father about it, and he said he had a right to it. Marriage is supposed to be a fifty-fifty proposition, he said."

Justin shook his head. "I mean, what do I care about a lamp? But he got riled up about it and kept sniping at my mom, so I said something nasty and he came at me and Zeus jumped him. I dragged Zeus out in the yard, and next thing I know my father's after me with the rifle to shoot my dog. He gets crazy when he loses his temper."

"And you pitched the gun into my yard?"

"Yeah." He grinned at me. "I had to get rid of it somewhere."

"I hid it for you," I said proudly. We'd finally reached my part of the saga.

Both Allison and Justin stopped and turned to stare at me.

"You did *what?*" Allison said.

"I hid Mr. Auerbach's gun. And he came and banged on my front door and then on my back door and Dolores never woke up. See, he knew I had it, but I lied and said I didn't. And he was so furious I was scared he'd break down the back door and come after me."

"He's not that crazy," Justin said. ". . . I don't think," he added.

I wasn't reassured because Justin didn't know his father very well. "Anyway," I said. "Dolores knows where the gun is, and she promised not to let him get it."

I waited for Justin to tell me how wonderful I'd been, but he began clumping along again in silence, and Allison and I followed him.

"So you'll camp out until your mother sends a ticket?" I asked him.

"That's the plan."

"Suppose he gets it out of me, I mean, where you

are?" I said. I could imagine Mr. Auerbach twisting my already aching arms behind my back. Could I withstand torture for Justin? I didn't think so. I didn't think I could withstand torture for anyone. Pain scares me most of all.

"Maybe you shouldn't come with us, Suki. That way you won't know where Justin is," Allison said.

I stopped. This was my out. "You're right," I said.

"No, she's not," Justin said. He turned to me and said soberly, "You can't go home, Suki. Not until your parents are there. Dolores won't be able to keep my father from harassing you by herself."

"But my father's coming home today." I almost believed it; I wanted so bad for it to be true.

"When today?" Justin asked.

"Um, tonight, I think."

"Not good enough."

"What do you mean? You just said yourself your father's not crazy."

"But he's got a temper and he's angry," Justin said.

I squeaked in panic as if they were dragging me off to that tent in the woods by force. I had to do something and fast. "Ugh," I said. "Ugh." I dropped the arms of the wheelbarrow and clutched my stomach.

"What's the matter?" Justin asked.

"Stomachache," I whimpered. "Oh, it hurts."

"Cut it out, Suki," Allison said. "This is no time for dramatics. Justin's in serious trouble."

So was I. I couldn't spend a night in a tent in the

woods. I'd go mad with fear. I'd lie there waiting for a bear to crash into the tent, or a snake, or a rabid raccoon. I pressed my lips together as if I were in pain.

"Listen, Suki, if you're not feeling well we can hide what's in the wheelbarrow in a bush or something and come back for it later. You go to Allison's house and lie down," Justin said.

"I think I'll go home," I murmured weakly.

"But you can't do that," he said. "I just explained. It isn't safe."

"Suki," Allison said, "why are you doing this? You're not sick. You're just scared of camping out, aren't you?"

"Oh, she's *not* scared," Justin said. "Not Suki. You didn't see how brave she was last night, Allison."

Allison looked at me. I smiled at her proudly and straightened up a little. Justin had just said I was brave. He *did* appreciate what I'd done for him. All of a sudden I felt terrific. And why go home now when it was morning and I could spend a whole day with my Apollo? It didn't get dark until after eight o'clock. I could leave for home hours before that on some pretext or other.

"Actually, I'm feeling okay now," I said. Cough. Cough. "Whatever it was went away. I'll come with you, at least until my father's due back."

"Good," Justin said.

Allison raised an eyebrow, but she didn't say anything.

We entered the woods. That is, Allison pulled aside some wild grapevines and steered us through a labyrinth of underbrush beneath a mess of skinny trees with interlacing canopies. I didn't like the vines or the stickery bushes, and I didn't like the grassy spot the size of a small bedroom she led us to either.

"Here we are," she said. "It's completely hidden. The bike path is just over there." She pointed. "And the river's just past that. But you can't see anything."

She was right. We were surrounded by greenery, walled in by fluttery green leaves, and who knew what was hiding in them watching us?

"Perfect," Justin said. He and Allison began setting up the tent.

I must have looked dejected as I stood watching them because Justin said, "I'll be out of your hair in a few days, Suki."

And my life forever. My heart popped like a drop of water in hot grease. The misery of my aching muscles was nothing compared to what that reminder did to me.

Zeus had already made himself at home. He lay stretched out with his head on his paws, watching Allison and Justin work. I dropped down beside my buddy and leaned on his back for comfort, cautiously in case he didn't want me using him for furniture. Zeus gave me a friendly lick on my bare knee and whacked his tail against the ground once or twice in welcome.

"Nice doggie," I said, relaxing a little.

Justin glanced over his shoulder and smiled at us. I preened in his silent approval, pleased with myself for a change. After smacking a few mosquitoes I said, "I hope someone remembered bug juice."

"We're all out at my house," Allison said.

"Well, we have plenty," I said. "I guess I'll go get some."

"No, you won't, Suki. You stay here and I'll get it," Allison said.

A question I'd thought of before occurred to me and I asked it. "Justin, where did you spend the night?"

"In my father's house, in my own room. After I tossed the gun out of his yard, he told me to go to bed and he'd see me in the morning. I went, but I took Zeus with me to guard the bedroom door." Justin picked up a handy rock and began hammering in the pegs for the tent as if he were hammering his father.

I wondered if Mr. Auerbach would have a fit again when he realized Justin was gone. "I hope your father doesn't track you down here," I said.

"How could he, if even Dolores doesn't know Allison's camping spot?" Justin asked.

"Don't worry, Suki, you're safe here," Allison said.

But I didn't feel safe. "Your father didn't really expect you to shoot your dog, did he?" I asked Justin.

"I don't know what he expected," Justin said.

131

Neither did I know what Mr. Auerbach expected. I wished my father *were* coming home today. I wished my mother were coming with him. I wanted them *and* Dolores *and* the police to shield me from Justin's father. When my parents got angry, the worst they ever did was yell a little. The more I thought about it, the more nervous I got about how mad I'd made Mr. Auerbach by taking his gun. He could have another gun. Probably he did, and what if he was itching to use it on me?

Allison's camping spot was like being stuffed in green tissue paper packed in a box. I felt claustrophobic and kept my eyes peeled for signs of venomous snakes or hairy tarantulas. Not even a chickadee was in sight.

The mosquitoes had brought their relatives to feast on me. I smacked away at them. Allison and Justin had the tent raised now, and they didn't seem to be bothered by bugs. Ticks! There were bound to be ticks this time of the year. I jumped to my feet. I'd end up with Lyme disease for sure.

"Allison," I said, "would you go back to my house *now* and get the bug repellent and my jeans and a long-sleeved shirt? *Please.*"

"In a minute," she said. She and Justin were making the green sides of the tent taut. I dragged the sleeping bags inside it to get away from the insect battalion and dropped the flap that made a kind of screen at the open end just to see what it would be like inside. More claustrophobia. And it smelled musty. I didn't like the nylon sides being so thin either. When I crawled back out to ask if they couldn't surround the thing with boards or something more substantial, both Allison and Justin were gone. Before I could stop myself, I screamed.

Immediately they came crashing back through the bushes. "What's the matter?" they asked in unison.

"Where were you?" I demanded.

"Checking to see if the tent can be spotted from the bike path," Allison said.

"It's invisible," Justin assured me. "The only thing is, we won't be able to make a fire until it's dark. Somebody might see the smoke."

"I like cold tuna," I said while my heartbeat slowed. "And personally, I could live on peanut butter sandwiches for a week."

"I'll be back soon," Allison said as she prepared to go.

Something I'd noticed before suddenly struck me. "Allison," I asked. "How come we only have two sleeping bags?"

"One for Justin and one for you," she said. "I can't sleep out with you tonight. I told you, I have to be home for the relatives."

"I thought they were only staying at your house last night."

"They decided to leave Sunday."

"But I can't stay here alone," I blurted out.

"Justin and Zeus'll be with you. You'll be safe, Suki," Allison said.

"You're *not* scared of camping out, are you, Suki?" Justin asked as if it was impossible that I should be.

"Of course not," I said automatically.

"Good," Allison said, although I could tell by the glint in her eye that she didn't believe me. "I'll run up to your house. Be back soon."

"Tell Dolores I'm taking her advice about the stars," I quavered.

Without even asking me what I meant, Allison nodded and took off. I was alone in the woods with Justin. But it was daylight, so that was fine. Right? Right. But what was I going to do about tonight? Sneak home and risk bumping into Mr. Auerbach, or stay here and face worse? Like what if I moved in the night and Zeus thought I was an intruder and attacked? Or what if I stepped on him in the dark and he didn't know it was an accident and turned on me? But I'd hidden a gun for Justin. Sleeping in a tent for him couldn't be any more dangerous. Or could it?

The rug-shaped sky overhead was a fuzzy blue with a few wispy clouds threaded through it. It was the only comforting space in sight.

"Suki, do you mind if I read for a while?" Justin asked me.

He looked exhausted, which figured, considering what he'd been through. What could I say? Even though talking to him was my only reward for being here, I had to be cool. "Sure, go ahead," I said. "I wish I had something to read."

In a minute I did. Justin dug out a manual on knot tying from his duffle bag and gave me a couple of pieces of string. "Here you go, Suki. This should keep you busy."

Knot tying? How romantic! Oh, well, who knew when I'd be in the position of Ariadne, who gave her hero string to help him find his way out of the labyrinth. Might as well learn what I could so I'd be ready for the next emergency. I started in on my knot study.

Justin couldn't read all afternoon. And even if he could, he couldn't read in the dark. Then he'd have nothing to do but talk to me. Although since it was only about eleven in the morning, dark was a long way off. And by then I'd be too scared to pay attention to anything except what was going on in the bushes around us. I tied a half hitch and tangled the string up trying to figure out the next knot. Not that I really wanted to.

What was I doing here? I could hide out from Mr. Auerbach a lot more comfortably in my own house. But I didn't move. Justin was there and Allison wasn't. That made me the only siren on the rock. Now if I could only sing pretty!

Chapter 13

After giving up on the knot book, I napped in the tent for a while. Then I sat in the late afternoon sunshine rubbing Zeus's belly. He looked so silly on his back, with his paws flopped in the air, groaning with pleasure, that it tickled me. Justin's long, narrow face was still intent on his book instead of me, but I was happy being near him, and the wind shushing the leaves sounded friendlier. Birds I couldn't see chittered peacefully to each other. The ground where I sat had a sweet, mossy smell. The world was beautiful.

Until the light changed.

Suddenly it was amber, which meant it was getting late. Of course, I could just say I was leaving and start walking. Justin couldn't stop me. A sudden scritching noise in the bushes set my spine tingling. My eyes fixed on that flimsy green tent. A knife could slice through it easily. Or what if a tree fell over onto it and crushed me inside? Justin might be crushed with me, but I'd be too dead to care, or worse yet, maimed for life. It would be much more comfortable to curl up between my clean, peach-colored sheets and trust Dolores to keep me safe from Mr. Auerbach.

Besides, I had to go to the toilet and Allison's perfect camping spot didn't include plumbing. It had to be a quarter of a mile at least to the downstairs bathroom in her house. That's what I'd do. Ask her folks to let me use the bathroom and then call Dolores to come get me. I could lie on the backseat of the car and Dolores could sneak me into our garage. Then I could hide under my own bed in case Mr. Auerbach was really crazy enough to force his way past her into our house.

"Justin," I said, "I'm going up to Allison's house. It's an emergency."

He frowned. "My father'll be home from work and out looking for us by now, Suki. What's the emergency?"

"I have to go to the bathroom," I admitted.

He laughed as if he thought I was being funny. "Use the bushes. I'll wait in the tent until you're done."

"I can't do that. It's unsanitary," I said.

"Suki, be reasonable. The Indians did it. Backpackers do it. It's a normal part of camping out in the wilderness."

"There's nothing normal about camping out. I want a flush toilet."

He shook his head at me. "And here I thought I could depend on you."

"You can."

"Then give a whistle when you're done." Without further ado he took his book and himself into the tent, dropping the door flap shut behind him.

Finding myself alone in an alien place, I shuddered. "Zeus," I whispered to the dog, "don't you let any rabid raccoons get me with my pants down, okay?"

I eased myself into the shrubbery, sure I was about to get poison ivy on my bare butt. I didn't even know how to recognize it, except it had three leaves. But every weed in sight had at least three leaves. There was bound to be poison ivy anywhere I squatted. I pushed down my shorts. Bugs could be crawling up the grass blades that were tickling my bottom. The idea made my skin prickle. I brushed a hand over myself to get rid of the bugs and nearly unbalanced into the poison ivy. Or whatever was there. And ticks! What about ticks? They leaped on you from the tips of grasses. Odysseus didn't suffer more than I had by the time I'd finished.

"You can come out now," I said to Justin. It occurred to me that I should have run off while he was in the tent and told him later somebody had kidnapped me. Not that he would have been likely to believe me.

Zeus wagged his tail as his master reappeared. Justin glanced at him and said, "How about going for a walk on the bike path before it gets too dark, Suki?" Zeus perked up as if he'd understood the question.

"Now?" I stalled. "But what if we miss Allison? She should have come back with the bug repellent long ago."

"She can just leave the stuff here for us."

"You don't care if you miss her?"

His frown was puzzled. "Why should I? We just saw her this morning."

I was thrilled. If he were totally gone on Allison, he wouldn't want to miss even five minutes of her company. Still, the only place I really felt like walking was home. So I stalled some more. "What if we bump into your father? I mean, if he's out looking for you—"

"On the bike path this late? Not likely. Come on. I need exercise. Don't you?"

"Me?" I never needed exercise, but instead of admitting I was a total blob, I said, "Well, I stay in shape without it." I smiled, bracing myself for a smart remark about my rotundity, but I was relieved when he didn't tease me. Not that that was a good sign. Boys who liked Allison were always teasing her. . . . Unless Justin didn't know how to tease. After all, he was an only child. . . . Like me.

Justin was heading for the bike path with Zeus

right at his heels. "Wait for me," I cried and hurried after him.

Three guys in their late teens whizzed past us on Rollerblades. Otherwise the path was empty. The sky was red through the trees over the river, and the river was a mirror washed in pink and yellow. "Look!" I said as a great blue heron bent its neck into a U-turn to nab something in the water.

Justin whistled. "That's one big bird for this populated an area."

"Populated? We're in the woods."

He chuckled as if I'd said something funny. "Come out to Colorado and I'll show you woods," he said.

Through the trees to the right of us I could see the headlights of cars on Rosendale Road. Nevertheless, I said, "This is wilderness enough for me."

"It wouldn't be too bad if it had a mountain or two," he said.

"You really need mountains?"

"I like climbing them. Yeah. Besides, I get a charge from looking at them. Mountains are awesome."

"The Adirondacks are only an hour's drive north of us," I said. "They're kind of worn down by age, but you can get lost in them."

"You're not much of an outdoorsperson, are you, Suki?"

My heart sank. I'd failed to measure up to his standards. Miserably I admitted, "I'm sort of an

140

indoor person. Just give me somebody I can talk to and I'm happy."

"Yeah, well, I know what you mean," he said. "I can talk to my mother about most anything and that's— yeah . . . But Mom's also the one who taught me to rock climb and how to track animals in the snow."

"She sounds terrific."

"She is."

I tripped over a crack in the asphalt while trying to watch Justin's face in the dusky light. He gripped my arm, and my heart jolted to a stop. "What's the matter?" he asked me.

"Nothing," I said. My heart was palpitating maniacally because he was touching me. "You were saying about your mother."

"Yeah. The thing is, now she's got this guy in her life." He let go of my arm, and my heart simmered down.

"What don't you like about him?" I asked with interest. This was my kind of subject.

"I don't know." Justin waited for Zeus, who had lifted his leg against a tree. "He thinks I'm strange because I read a lot, and he's always boasting about the wild stuff he does—like jumping into burning forests and hanging out of helicopters to rescue hikers lost in the snow."

"But you like rock climbing. That sounds just as wild to me."

Justin laughed. "Yeah, but he makes me feel wimpy,

141

like I need to cut loose from my mother and join a motorcycle gang or something. He talks to me like— it's hard to explain."

"The guy puts you down?"

Justin shrugged. "Well, it feels that way to me."

"So what does your mother say?"

"Not much. She figures how we get along is between him and me. I guess it is." Zeus bumped his hand, and Justin rested it on the dog's head. "That's why I left. I didn't want to get into it with him and mess things up for her. I mean, she's happy with him." He shook his head. "I didn't realize that she wasn't happy until she met him and I saw how happy she could be. . . . I'm not making sense, am I?" His expression was lost in the shadows of the trees, but I could hear his hurt and confusion.

"Sure you are," I said. His mother was his best friend, and that guy was taking her away from Justin. As tactfully as I could, I asked him, "Doesn't anybody you like live near you in Colorado?"

"No. We live ten miles up a hiking trail that's only used by backpackers. I see people when we go into town for supplies or a movie, but not long enough to make friends with them."

"How about pen pals then?"

"I had a couple from the school I went to in Wyoming, but you know how it is. After a while they stop writing back."

"Really? I guess most people think writing letters is a chore, but I love it."

He chuckled. "I bet you write letters as easily as you talk."

"You think I talk too much?" I asked. A crescent moon over the river wasn't lighting up the navy blue sky too well.

"I think you're a talented talker," he said.

Was that a compliment? Or was there a sly criticism in it? I wasn't sure. In school my hand's up first when it comes to interpreting a poem or a story, but the meanings in real life are harder. Sometimes I think school smarts don't have much to do with real life.

A family on bikes and trikes sped past us as if they were late for dinner. I wished I were home eating my dinner, even one of Dolores's. I shivered, not that it was cold, but I was crawly with nerves. Plus I hadn't eaten anything since breakfast. "I'm hungry," I said.

"Okay. Let's go light the fire and cook those turkey dogs you brought," he said.

Now was the time to tell Justin that my father had surely arrived and I had to go home. Or I could say I didn't feel well and leave. I actually didn't feel too well. But he was talking to me the way I'd imagined he might if I stayed, and I didn't want to leave him now.

Our campsite had disappeared into blackness, but Zeus turned off the bike path into the bushes as if he knew where he was going and Justin followed him. I grabbed his hand so as not to be left behind. He led me through the underbrush without comment, but when we got to the dome shaped shadow of the tent, he said, "How come your hand's so cold?"

"I don't feel very well," I said and shivered convincingly.

"I'll get you my jacket." He ducked into the tent.

I was alone in the dark. Something was sticking into my ankle, and I was afraid to look down and see what it was. I could hear things, leaves talking about me, bats plotting to land in my hair. "Justin, I need a nightlight!" I yelled.

"Shush." He dropped something warm around my shoulders. "Are you scared?"

I was shaking hard from either fear or malaria. "I've never camped out before," I said. "My parents head for motels when we travel."

"You've never camped out? No kidding!" He bent to light the fire he'd already set up. I watched the flare-up of a newspaper torch highlight his cheekbones and thought of Prometheus and fire. Somehow everything about Justin was heroic.

He got the fire going quickly. Fire was how people kept wild animals away, I told myself. And at least now I could see the ground around me—sort of. Justin stuck the turkey dogs on sticks and began toasting them.

"Allison's family camps," I confided, promoting

144

her to punish myself for being such a wimp. "They ski together and go canoeing." He and Allison were made for each other. I had to face reality. Maybe they'd invite me to their wedding someday. It would be a tragic occasion for me, but I would smile through my tears, as they say.

"Does she read?" he asked.

"Allison? Sure," I said. "Well, actually, only when she has to. She doesn't get lost in books exactly."

"I read a lot. Sci-fi, mostly," Justin said. "And encyclopedias. Mom got an old set of encyclopedias at an auction once, and I read my way through to the *Ms*."

"How come you stopped?"

"A porcupine got the rest."

"Oh, sure."

"No, really. We were gone for a while, and when we got back there were just shreds of covers left."

I laughed, but I glanced over my shoulder, wondering if there were porcupines in these woods.

He laughed, too. "It was a drag. I was really into finishing the whole alphabet."

The trees were definitely leaning in on us. Zeus nuzzled my hand. I jumped and yipped until I realized who it was and wrapped my arms around him for comfort.

"Suki, Suki, Suki. . . . " The voice sounded familiar.

"Justin, I think that's Dolores calling me."

"Let's go see," he said.

I grabbed hold of his sleeve, and Zeus and I followed Justin back through the underbrush to the bike path. There was Dolores with a flashlight in one hand and a bulging plastic shopping bag in the other.

"What are you doing here?" I asked.

"Your friend came. She said you need things."

"But why did you come instead of Allison, Dolores?"

"She had to go home. She tell me how to find you. She say to just keep calling."

Zeus suddenly took off down the bike path after something and Justin charged after the dog, yelling for him to come back. I took advantage of his distraction to whisper to Dolores, "I'm not all right. I'm scared. Tell Justin I have to go home with you because my dad's looking for me, okay?" I slapped at a mosquito.

"I brought the bug killer." She took it out of the bag.

"Good! So how about it?"

"Better if you stay," Dolores said slowly.

"I don't think so," I said. "Has Justin's father come to our house yet?"

Dolores shook her head.

"Well, even if I'm there when he comes, you can just say I'm gone, and I'll hide in a closet."

"Better if you're not there," Dolores said.

"But I can't *sleep* here, Dolores."

"You like this boy?"

I nodded.

"He don't try to touch or grab at you like—you know?"

"Of course not. Anyway, he likes Allison," I said.

"But you are here with him, not her," Dolores said.

What she meant was this was my chance to change Justin's mind. Dolores was no oracle. She was Aphrodite in disguise. Of course I had to stay. What kind of Greek hero gives up the quest out of fear of the dark? If I wasn't brave enough to camp out with Justin, I didn't deserve to be invited to his wedding to Allison.

Just then Justin returned with Zeus.

Dolores handed him the can of bug spray. While doing that, she lowered the flashlight and I thought I saw something skitter across the path. I screamed. I couldn't help it.

"What's wrong, Suki?" Justin asked.

"I saw a creature," I whispered.

He shook his head. "I can't believe this kid," he said to Dolores. "Every little thing scares her. I mean, considering how scared she is, she's really brave to even be here."

I moaned a little and sidled closer to Zeus. Dolores handed the plastic bag to Justin, and he moved back toward the fire. "I'll see you tomorrow, Dolores," I whispered, ". . . if I survive."

Chapter 14

$\mathcal{J}$ found Justin standing next to the fire, rubbing bug repellent on his arms and neck. He handed the can to me, and I sprayed myself liberally, even though the mass attack of the whining insects seemed to be over now that the sun was down. Also in the plastic bag were pants and a long-sleeved shirt for me. Best of all, Dolores had included the book of Greek myths I'd had on my night table.

I ducked into the tent to put on more clothes and sat down on a flashlight on top of a sleeping bag. Would it keep Justin awake if I used the light to read? I knew I wouldn't be able to sleep surrounded by the noisy creatures of the night that were already scritching and scratching and zinging out there. And the flashlight had other possible uses. If worst came to worst, I could bop a bear over the nose before it ate me. As to any smaller creature with teeth—maybe I could throw the book at it to stun it and then smother it in Allison's sleeping bag.

Justin had rescued the turkey dogs before they burned, and they smelled smoky and delicious. I wrapped mine in a slice of oatmeal bread and promptly scorched my tongue when I took a bite. "Hot," I complained.

"Do we have any mustard?" Justin asked.

"No. Do you usually on your camp-outs?"

"Me? Mostly I eat whatever we can catch and kill."

I shuddered. Justin, the mountain man! "Personally, I like civilized food, preferably served in a restaurant with a big dessert menu."

"You think turkey dogs are civilized?"

"At least they don't have fur and drip blood."

"I bet your friend Allison's not so fussy," Justin said.

That stung. "So what," I said. "She's probably watching TV with Toad right now while I'm roughing it here with you."

He smiled. "Being brave is easier when you're mad, isn't it?"

"Don't get me too mad," I said. "I might sic Zeus on you."

He chuckled, a cute kind of sound that I wanted to hear again. "Considering how terrific you were with the rifle last night, I don't know where I come off razzing you about bravery," he said.

"I was brave, wasn't I?" I said with a satisfaction that made him laugh at me.

"Actually," I told him, "this turkey dog is cooked to perfection. Can I have another?"

After our supper, we sat there studying what we could see of the stars and speculating about intelligent life in other galaxies. Allison doesn't believe there is any, but Justin and I assumed there had to be. With billions of stars out there, it's unlikely that we're unique. It was cozy that we agreed on something and thrilling to be alone with him, but I was wishing I were Allison so that he'd want to put his arm around me. As it was I was only Suki, so I sat on the damp ground in the chilly night air and shivered.

The fire turned to embers, and I could feel eyes watching us from the woods. I couldn't *see* any eyes, but I could hear creatures making eerie squeaks and squeals. "I think I'll turn in," I said when I couldn't stand it another second.

I dove into the tent, wriggled into Allison's sleeping bag, and flicked on the flashlight. I didn't like being inside the tent much, but it wasn't as crawly with possibilities as the woods were, and it was a whole lot warmer. I opened my book. The flashlight lit up the pages just enough to read by. If I could read, I could forget where I was.

"Hey," Justin said when he joined me in the tent. "Are you planning to hog that light, or do I get to read, too?"

I glared at him. "I have to read myself to sleep."

"Yeah? So do I. How about if we read to each other?"

What a thrilling suggestion! I promptly read to him about how Hermes taught Apollo to play the lyre, and how, in exchange, Apollo brought him to Mount Olympus and introduced him to Zeus. When it was Justin's turn, he read to me about some alien planet where the people were just pulsating brains. Yuck. Isn't this world scary enough without inventing even worse ones? I watched his face as he read and imagined we were under an olive tree on some sunburned Greek island and that Justin's golden chariot and lyre were waiting just outside the tent. The god Apollo had been not only beautiful, but also gentle and kind—at least when he got older.

Imagining that Justin was Apollo, I thought how thrilling it would be if he kissed me, just a goodnight peck, even a brotherly one. Or what if I kissed him? A quick press of my lips against his cheek and then I'd dive under my sleeping bag and never have to know his reaction. I mean, what if he wiped it off? I'd be humilated for life.

"So what do you think?" he asked me.

"About what?"

"What I just read to you, Suki."

"Oh," I said. "It was great."

"You weren't listening, were you?"

I pretended to yawn. "I'm sort of tired. It's been a long day."

151

"Yeah. It has. Well, good night," he said. He put the book down, turned off the flashlight, and pulled his sleeping bag up around his ears. His back was to me. Without the flashlight, all I could see was the dark hill of his shoulder. I closed my eyes and began a daydream about Justin taking me in his arms and me waking up to find his lips on mine. "Mmm," I moaned.

"What?" he asked.

"Nothing," I said.

I heard him moving around. "There's a root under this sleeping bag," he said.

"I can shove over some," I said and pressed myself into the side of the tent to give him room, but then a rock stuck into my hip. I moved back and bumped into him.

"Sorry," he said and rolled away from me as if I'd scorched him.

I sighed.

"Good night," he said.

"Night," I told him and regrouped my daydream.

I must have fallen asleep in the middle of it because suddenly I was awake. Something had dropped onto the tent. "What was that?" I screeched, grabbing for the body next to mine, which happened to be Justin's.

"Um?" he mumbled sleepily.

"Something's attacking us." Zeus began to bark, so I knew I was right. Justin pried my arms off him and unzipped our front door.

"Don't go out there," I said. "What if it's a bear?"

"Flashlight," he said and came back for it. He left the flap open when he exited the tent. That left me exposed to whatever wanted to get in. I snailed up small in the middle of Allison's sleeping bag, hoping the bear would take a mouthful of it instead of me when it bit.

"Just a twig, Suki," I heard Justin say a few minutes later.

I peeked out at him, but the flashlight was shining in my eyes. He aimed it at the small branch in his hand. "See, just a twig," he assured me. Then he shut off the flashlight and pitched himself back into his sleeping bag.

Of course, I knew he was lying. That little branch couldn't have made such a noise. And Justin had left the door unzipped. And I wasn't about to risk getting up and zipping it shut. He was breathing so evenly I figured he was sound asleep. Did I dare to wake him up to close the door? I couldn't fall asleep while it was open, I told myself. Except I must have. Eventually. Because next time I opened my eyes it was morning.

✳✳✳

Justin and I were eating cereal straight out of the little boxes and chatting about our favorite breakfast foods—mine being Belgian waffles with strawberries and whipped cream and his being scrambled eggs and sausage—when his father appeared. Justin froze, and I dropped my box and spattered milk over my sweatshirt. Seeing the squirrel shooter standing there at the edge of our campsite scared me more than any imaginary bears.

Zeus stood up and kind of leaned forward as if he didn't know whether to wag his tail or growl.

"Sit, Zeus," Justin said, and he rose to his feet. Grudgingly, the dog obeyed. I scooted to Zeus's side and slung my arms around his strong neck for safety's sake—mine, not his.

Mr. Auerbach didn't take his eyes off Justin. "I called your mother," he said.

"You did?"

"I told her about what happened and that you'd run off."

"How did you find me?" Justin asked.

"Never mind that," his father said. "Your mother wants you to come home. . . . I expect you want to go."

Justin nodded.

"All right." Mr. Auerbach's voice was heavy with resignation. "I'll get you and the dog on the next available flight out."

Father and son both kept standing there not saying anything, not looking at each other. It seemed like they might call it quits without another word, so I said hastily, "You wouldn't really have shot Zeus, would you, Mr. Auerbach?"

His eyes went to his son, but he answered me. "I was trying to teach him a lesson. He brought the dog into my house. He was responsible for controlling the animal."

"But you were just bluffing with the gun, weren't you?" I persisted.

Mr. Auerbach looked at me for the first time since he'd appeared. "I knew Justin wouldn't shoot his dog, if that's what you mean," he said quietly. "He'd have been more likely to turn the gun on me."

"Justin wouldn't have done that. He's not violent," I said with a certainty that quickly turned into doubt. My Apollo didn't seem to be violent, but then I didn't know anybody who was, so how could I tell?

"I shouldn't have threatened him," Mr. Auerbach was saying in a flat, sad voice. "The dog attacked me, but I shouldn't have brought out a gun."

More silence. Mr. Auerbach looked so haunted that I almost felt sorry for him. Justin wasn't helping any, so I tried again. "I guess you could have gotten along okay if Zeus hadn't made you mad," I said.

"It wasn't just the dog," Justin's father said quietly. "Nothing turned out right. They both got under my skin." His shoulders slumped and his eyes dropped.

"I wanted it to work out, too," Justin said. "I mean, I wanted to find out about you."

"Your mother told me once that I'd be better off living alone," Mr. Auerbach said. "I don't get along with people that well. I don't—but you're my son and I thought maybe you were old enough so that we'd understand each other."

"Mom said you were a decent person," Justin said.

"I'm sorry," Mr. Auerbach said, and now his voice was lumpy with emotion. "I'm sorry." He shook his head and turned so we couldn't see his face.

Chapter 15

Justin and his father were so rigid standing there that I was afraid they might shatter into pieces. Zeus made a sound like a whimper in the back of his throat. Abruptly Justin dropped to his knees and put his arms around his dog.

"You might as well come back to the house until it's time to go, Justin," Mr. Auerbach said finally. "I'll help carry this stuff."

"Good idea," I said to encourage Justin to accept.

But he ignored me. "I can cart it back by myself," he told his father.

"Whatever you want," Mr. Auerbach said.

"I could help you, Justin," I offered, reluctantly because my arms still ached from yesterday's hauling.

"No, you go ahead home, Suki," Justin said. "I'll see you before I go, okay?"

"Okay."

My heart had sunk so low when Justin said the word "go" that I barely felt it jump when Mr. Auerbach said to me, "I'll give you a ride home, and you can return my rifle."

"I'm not returning it yet," I blurted, afraid of what he might do. Then I held my breath and waited for the explosion.

None came. Mr. Auerbach simply sighed and nodded sadly. "All right," he said. "My car's in the bike trail parking lot if you want a ride anyway." And he started off, head down.

I looked at Justin. He was grinning. "Not bad, Suki," he said admiringly. "Not bad."

"But your father feels awful," I said. "I think I should talk to him." And I used what energy I had left to chase after Mr. Auerbach and ask him to wait a minute for me. Then I ducked back into the tent to get the bag with my toilet kit and change of clothes. Justin was already busy breaking camp.

"See you," I said before leaving, to remind him that he'd said he would stop by my house.

Mr. Auerbach was a fast walker. I had all I could do to keep up with him on the bike path heading toward the parking lot by the old railroad station. We covered the distance in five minutes, and I didn't manage to catch my breath until I was sitting beside him in his car.

"Justin's a really nice boy," I said as we turned onto Rosendale Road.

"I suspect he is."

"He likes writing letters," I said. "Maybe if you write to each other?"

Mr. Auerbach's cheek twitched, and I realized he was crying. It confused me to have the first real-life bad guy I'd ever met turn so pitiful. In stories a villain can be counted on to stay evil so you can comfortably hate him. Anyway, I shut up, because even *I* didn't feel equal to chatting with a grown man in tears.

"Don't worry," he said to me when he dropped me off at my house. "There won't be any more trouble."

I thanked him for the ride and waved good-bye. What I'd do about the gun, I decided, was wait until Justin was safely gone and my father was home, and then invite Mr. Auerbach over to pick it up.

I went directly to the kitchen to tell Dolores the latest.

"Too bad," she said when I'd finished.

"What's too bad?"

"Your boyfriend goes so far away now."

"He's not my boyfriend," I said. "He didn't even try to kiss me."

"He is shy maybe," Dolores said. "He needs to get older."

I hugged her for offering that excuse even though I thought Justin wouldn't have been too shy to kiss Allison if she'd been the one to stay. It wasn't that he didn't like me. He liked me okay, but I obviously didn't make him quiver and shake and melt in the middle, which was what he did to me.

It felt good to shower and get into clean clothes after my camping experience. Besides, the morning was too warm for a long-sleeved shirt and long pants.

Allison called while I was brushing my hair. "Did you make it through the whole night out there?" she asked me.

"Of course," I said coolly.

"Oh, Suki," she crooned. "I'm so proud of you. I figured you'd do it for Justin if you were ever going to do it at all."

"Do what?"

"Camp out. I could have joined you, you know. My mother didn't need me last night, but I wanted to give you time alone with him."

"You did that deliberately?" Trickery wasn't Allison's style. She must have learned it from me. "Well, thanks, but it didn't work," I said.

"What do you mean it didn't work? You camped out in the woods and made friends with a dog, a big dog. Aren't you pleased with yourself?"

"I guess I am," I said. But what I'd done hadn't sunk in yet. There were other things to think about— like Justin.

"So what happened last night?" Allison asked me next.

"Nothing much," I told her. "No bears, no kisses.

We just went to sleep. His father came by this morning and said he was sorry. Justin's going to fly home on the next plane out of here."

"Whew, that's good news."

"It is?"

"Sure, because I thought Eric might have gotten Justin murdered or something. You know, it was Eric who told Mr. Auerbach how to find the camping area."

"Your *brother* spilled the beans? I don't understand."

"Well, I biked to your house yesterday to get the stuff you asked for, but Dolores insisted she'd bring it. I guess she wanted to make sure you were okay, and I figured it was all right to tell her how to find you. I mean, she swore she'd never give the location away."

"She wouldn't have," I said.

"Yeah, but then I went home, and Justin's father must have followed me because he pulled in our driveway right behind me and tried to convince me he needed to speak to his son. He was even going to write a message for me to deliver when I wouldn't tell him where to find Justin. Then along comes big-mouth Eric, and he tells Mr. Auerbach how to find the campsite. Can you believe it?"

"So how did you know I was home?"

"I found the sleeping bag and tent and stuff on the patio, and I saw Justin hiking up the road with Zeus."

"He didn't speak to you?"

"I told you, I just saw him leaving. I didn't talk to him."

"Allison, do you like him a lot?" I asked.

"Well, sure I like him. He's a nice kid. I mean, I don't like him the way you like him, but I like him okay."

I sighed with relief. She wasn't going to take him away from me, at least not deliberately. "If only I looked like you so Justin would fall for me," I said.

"Suki, don't be stupid. Think of all the married ladies you see who aren't good-looking at all. Their husbands had to have picked them for what's inside them."

I wavered. "Do you think Justin likes what's inside me?"

"Why not? I do," Allison said.

Sometimes she can be such a good friend. I was feeling better when suddenly it hit me. It didn't matter whether he liked me or not. My Apollo, my mountain man, was moving out of my life on the next plane. "But Allison, I'll never see him again," I moaned.

"He'll come back."

"Why should he?"

"To see you."

"Are you crazy?"

"All right, to visit his father, then," she said.

I must have lost track of the conversation about

162

then because when I tuned in again, Allison was saying, " . . . so if we go, do you want to come with us?"

"Go where?"

"Suki, what's the matter with you? I told you. Camping. My mother said I could invite you to go camping with us in August."

"Oh," I said. "I don't know, Allison. I'll think about it." At that moment my front doorbell rang and my stomach lurched. "Talk to you later. Bye," I said. And for once *I* hung up on Allison.

Chapter 16

$\mathcal{J}$ raced downstairs to open the door, and there stood Justin with Zeus at his side.

"Came to say good-bye," he said. "My father's got me booked on a three o'clock plane." He handed me the plastic bags of food I'd brought to his campsite and smiled.

"Did you and your father talk any more?"

"Sort of," Justin said. "We agreed it was too bad I didn't get a chance to see much of the countryside around here. He said I should come back someday."

"So it's okay between you?"

"Not okay, but better, thanks to you."

"To me?"

"Yeah, you broke the ice this morning. I was glad you were there. In fact, I don't know how to thank you for all you've done for me, Suki. You're an awesome girl and, considering what a scaredy-cat you are, you're brave, too." The grin on his face told me

164

he was joking about the brave part, but I pretended to myself that he had meant it.

"Thanks," I said. Then to keep from bursting into tears, I knelt down and hugged Zeus. "Good-bye, good buddy. You're my first doggie friend," I told him. Zeus licked my chin.

"Tell Allison I said good-bye," Justin said. "Tell her thanks, too, and say good-bye to Dolores for me." He hesitated. "I'll write you. Okay?"

I was still kneeling at his feet with my arms around Zeus. Justin didn't budge, so I stood up, hoping maybe this was it—the moment of the farewell kiss. But he took a step back and said, "Well, so good-bye."

"Bye, Justin." The tears welled up, and I had to turn away to hide my face because it squinches into a monster mask when I cry. I left the door standing wide open and dashed up to my room, where I threw myself on the bed and bawled full out.

When I finally got control of myself and went back downstairs, Justin had gone. I shut and locked the front door and went to find Dolores. She was packing. Mrs. Esposito was returning tomorrow. My father would be home tonight.

"Oh, Dolores, I'll miss you!" I wailed, and I meant it.

"Never mind. I visit with you on Sundays when I come to pick up my sister for her day off," she told me. "I don't forget you." Then she rocked me in her arms, squeezing hard, and she was every bit as comforting as Mrs. Esposito could have been.

Dad came home that night and brought me a stuffed mule from California, toy-sized of course. I guess I must have looked puzzled at his choice of gift because he said, "His expression got to me, Suki."

The mule was showing teeth and tongue in a wide-open hee-haw. It was really ugly. "Oh, sure! Thanks, Daddy," I told him and kissed his plump cheeks. His mustache tickled me as usual.

We stayed up past midnight talking about what had happened to each of us the past week. When I got to my part in the scene with the gun, Dad turned white and I had to assure him that Mr. Auerbach wasn't crazy, just kind of awkward emotionally. It took a while to convince Dad that we were safe living next door to Justin's father, but I did finally. My father's a love, even if his taste in gifts is weird, and I was really glad to have him home and very glad to have him be my father instead of somebody difficult like Mr. Auerbach.

Mrs. Esposito came home, too, and brought me a conch shell, which I put on my Olympic deity shelf to represent Poseidon, god of the sea. She seemed pleased that I'd gotten along so well with her sister. "One Sunday you come home with us to meet the family," she said. And then she told me about her grandchildren and how smart the littlest girl was. "She know everything, Suki, just like you."

So many compliments had come my way that I was beginning to think I must be okay—not perfect like Allison, but pretty good at least. Certainly I had more courage than I'd given myself credit for.

***

I invited Mr. Auerbach over the following Saturday and left him sitting in the living room with my father while I went down to the basement to get his rifle from behind the furnace. Dad had agreed that was as good a place as any to leave it, and he hadn't even wanted to look at it.

When I got back upstairs with the gun, my father and Mr. Auerbach were discussing some change in a zoning ordinance that would prevent home owners from keeping trailers on their properties. Neither of them seemed very worked up about it. I handed the rifle to Mr. Auerbach, and he asked, "Do you think Justin would like to own this, Suki?"

"I don't know," I said. "He told me he hunts." I looked at my father to see what he thought about that. He raised an eyebrow and grimaced.

"I could give it to him for Christmas," Mr. Auerbach was saying.

When he stood up to go, his face spread in a smile that reminded me of Justin's. He surprised me by confiding, "You were right. It would have gone better if Justin hadn't brought the dog with him. Dogs make me nervous."

"They do?" I reached out my hand to hold him back. I wanted to tell him about how I'd gotten over being scared of Zeus. But my father shook his head at me and proceeded to usher Mr. Auerbach and his rifle out the front door.

"Well, he's not as uptight as I thought he was," Dad said after he returned.

"I could help that man, Dad," I said. "If *I* can get over being afraid of dogs, anyone can." I was thinking of Allison's wild animal taming advice.

"Ah, the zeal of the converted!" my father said.

"What's that mean?"

"That before you go to work on our neighbor, you better find out if he wants to get over his fear."

"You're right, Dad," I said. It occurred to me that even if Justin didn't like me except as a friend, he had given me something important. He'd been the reason I'd tried to make friends with Zeus and the reason I'd dared to spend the night camping in the woods.

He'd changed my life—not the way I'd thought I wanted, but certainly for the better. I'd been caged by my fears and he'd sprung the lock, he and Allison, with some help from Dolores and the Greek gods. I might even be able to accept the invitation to go camping with Allison's family in August. Why not?

✳✳✳

Justin's letter came the next day. It said that he and Zeus had gotten home fine, and his mother had been really happy to have him back. He went on to tell me that Zeus had chased a bear away from their cabin, and that he'd decided he could put up with his mother's boyfriend since she was happy with the guy. "How about we do a cookout on our campsite for old time's sake when I come back to visit my father?" he wrote. And he signed himself, "Your friend, Justin."

He was coming back! My mood bounced sky-high. Immediately, I got out my purple pen and lavender stationery and started writing.

"Dear Justin," I wrote. "You said I did a lot for you. Well, you did more for me. Like I'm thinking of camping with Allison's family in August. Can you believe it?

"Oh, and a poodle jumped out of the window of a car at the gas station and ran past me and I didn't faint or get hysterical. Thank Zeus for me for that, and tell him I miss him."

I thought of the bone from the butcher that I'd never given Zeus. I could buy him a rawhide bone and send it to him. That would give him something to remember me by. I knew I'd never forget him, or his master.

Then I told Justin about his father saying he was scared of dogs. "I'm thinking of starting conversations with him when he's working in his garden. Maybe I can convince him that if he faced his fear, he could overcome it. I'll keep you posted on how that comes out," I wrote.

And when Justin returned, I would try singing my siren song again. Who knew, this time he might hear me. I eyed my gods of Olympus stage set. I'd asked for courage and found it. What if I tried giving Aphrodite a pomegranate instead of an ordinary apple? Love couldn't be any harder to get than courage, could it? Anyway, it was worth a try.